The Golden Debt

Anthology

Desirée Jaeckel

Enjoy!

Desirée Jaeckel

CONTENTS

THE GOLDEN DEBT

CHAPTER 1

The shadows were growing long, as was the Renaissance. It was an age that would soon lead to enlightenment. Light was playing tricks on the coming night, but in the Dutch town of Delft, the dark was not easily fooled. The artist was walking slowly, painstakingly like he painted. The colors of the girl swirled and teased every thought. Red madder were her lips, wide eyes blending brown and yellow ochre in perfect harmony. Johannes Vermeer splashed through the muddy half -frozen puddles without care. He would finally be rid of the debt that hung around his neck like the anchor of a tall ship. Until today, he had been obsessed with the riddance of it. His studio was the only oasis where he could find relief. He had actually compromised his creative values and tried to speed up the process. Painting himself into "The Procuress" meant he could do with one less model. He had completed this in record time; usually it took him at least a year to finish. His work was not like God's creation taking only six days. His genius was not timed like some dog race. Each stroke was thought out and plotted, tenderly painted on the canvas. He laid his foundation like the masons who worked on Notre Dame. One error would cause his entire work to come tumbling down and he did not like to fail in his artistic endeavors.

He could not believe how perfect the timing was. His mother, Digna, had recently brought a young girl to work and live at her inn, the Mechelen. Fleur was so enchanting; he wished he could paint her the moment he laid his eyes on her. He was drawn to her, but was in no position to act on his desires. Now Pieter had come to him with the perfect solution. When he met with Pieter early today he seemed almost alien. Vermeer had never seen his best friend in such a dark mood. Always a lively fellow Pieter had not a care in the world. He was quite enviable. Not only was he rich and handsome he was extremely likable. When Pieter spoke, his words poured out like a beautiful waterfall. "I have a way to lift the burden of your debt to me completely. Our actions must be shrouded in secrecy and you will follow my instruction to the letter." The artist was curious, but more excited about the possibility of cleaning the slate that kept him up at night. Pieter could not wait to continue, "You have seen the new tavern girl at the Mechelen." Vermeer's heart stopped beating for just a second. "Johannes, you are my best friend and I trust you completely. You are discreet and it is important when friends share their souls." Johannes waited patiently for Pieter to continue. "I must have her with me now and always, Johannes, she is my natural daughter. More of one than Magdalena could ever be. I would swim to the new world and back to make this right, to go back in time and rearrange my life. I would change decisions I made based on greed and the immaturity of a young man who feared his father and poverty. I tell you she is the perfect combination of all the good in her mother, Tessa and me. Yet, I have to admit she looks much like I did at her age. It is uncanny and I can hardly grasp what I have discovered. The love I have for Tessa still burns bright. It rages like it did all those years ago. I am blinded by the double light of Tessa and Fleur. The years have played a dirty trick on me. They have stolen my lover and a child more beautiful than the azure sky and cinnamon sunsets of Holland that bid me goodnight on the best of days. I want you to paint her, Vermeer, so I may always gaze on her lovely face. And if you do this we will be even on every score. You will owe nothing but the portrait."

Vermeer was in shock; his tongue was glued to his teeth. This was a secret of an epic size. Maria, Pieter's wife must never learn the truth. She was a dangerous woman. Her fortune matched her powers with a family wealthier than Pieter's, which was hard to fathom. This is why the marriage had been arranged. His family had wanted to rise to the top of society in Delft and the marriage had accomplished their goal. It was sad to think of the terrible cost it was for Pieter; parents sometimes did not stop and think of these aspects when arranging marriages that would put their family at an advantage. If she would discover any of this there would be hell to pay all the way around. Maria would destroy everything in her path. Pieter waited patiently for him to reply realizing his friend was too dumbfounded to speak. Vermeer seemed very skeptical, but was hoping it was all true. Vermeer could not get the words out and had to take a deep inhale before continuing. "Perhaps you are mistaken. You have drunk one too many of your own fine ales. They have worked on your mind like a witch's potion. What proof has you?" Pieter looked off into the distance. Then his last words came out like a stone that fell from the highest cliff into the waters of a frigid sea. "The pearl earrings!"

CHAPTER 2

Tessa never wore them. Like seashells buried in the dark warm waters of the Caribbean they hid quietly in her carved box since Fleur was born. They could only remind her of Pieter and it was too painful to think of him. As she lay dying they weighed heavily on her mind, as did the man she desperately loved and had stayed true to all of these years. A year ago he had walked past her stall in the market, lightening was crackling between them. The thunderous pleasure echoed to the forbidden past. It lasted only a moment and he was gone. Their love had been all encompassing and complete, yet it was not enough to break the unspoken rules of seventeenth century Holland.

She was young. Pieter was ten years her senior, but as lively as a teenager. His energy was boundless. He loved to tell her funny stories and was very positive about everything in the world. "Tessa," he would say in his effervescent voice, "we will be together, I swear, just love me now and you will see. The entire Spanish Fleet cannot stop me." Delft was busy growing then, especially the marketplace. She had her little wheelbarrow selling flowers all around the town. She could barely live on those humble earnings, but she had her youth and beauty. This was all he needed. Every day for months he would buy one rose from her. She was charmed and he was full of as much charisma as a dozen red ones in full bloom. She felt like a wilted tulip when he left her standing there as her eyes followed him like an eagle soaring in the air until not even a speck remained.

One day he brought his personal carriage without a driver. He swept her away past the fishmonger's smells and butcher's stare. The country was buzzing with life and there under a blue sky hidden in a copse of trees, they created Fleur out of the magic that had been brewing that long summer day. But he was a rich man whose parents insisted he have a richer wife. Maria was from one of the wealthiest trading families on the continent. It was whispered they had made a good portion of their money from the slave trade. Maria was educated, but very ignorant when it came to the plight of her fellow man. She wore beautiful clothing, but they could not make her so. She rode thoroughbred horses, but never gave them a bale of hay or helped in their care in any way. She lived in an ostentatious house with huge windows that looked out upon Delft, but not once did she clean them. Her parents' country manor spread across hundreds of acres, but she never spent time in the cutting gardens. She assumed the gardener would bring the flowers to the servants who daily freshened up the numerous vases that were set in great variety around every room. When Maria walked through the marketplace in her finest garments her head was held high and she did not see the condition of the poor nor did she care to. She did not give a fig about the squalor they endured, for Maria would always be satisfied and satiated every living moment and Pieter would be hers. There was no doubt. Her cold eyes looked upon the river, but could not see the depth. Only the reflection of a face her money could not alter. Beauty was the one thing that eluded her.

The child was growing inside Tessa like a loud whisper. The days went by like a play. She felt like an actress in a musical. Every hour there was a song in her heart. Before Pieter found out he was going to be forced to marry Maria he was so excited about their love. He never thought ahead. Pieter was just living in the precious moments they shared. He purchased a small stand for her and watched as she delighted in her trade. She loved being a florist and they were happy together. But the cold winter was coming and the icy winds would blow across their lives. One day it ended and the agony seemed greater than all of the pleasures. She was gathering carnations and arranging them in a perfect art creation. Artistic by nature, her crafty hands and eyes worked together like a paint and brush. Pieter walked up to the stand and looked like death. Instantly she knew. She had not told him about the child, the moment had not yet been perfect enough. Her inner fears were holding back the truth like a dam about to burst. He claimed his parents would disinherit him. They would strip him of any means to give her a comfortable life. They would never speak to him again and also make sure he could never make his living in Holland. He did not like or love Maria, but the hand had been dealt and the winnings collected by his parents many years ago without his consent or knowledge. His parents had struck the bargain from hell. Tears could not come, only pain that seared her womb like a fire that could not be quenched. "Tessa, you must have these. I want you to wear them always and feel the weight of them like the weight of our love."

He placed a pair of radiant and precious pearl earrings upon her. They stung more than pleased. Their glitter seemed false to her; their worth less than the mud in a pig sty. She stood like a statue in the square, with even less feelings. Then he was gone.

She never wore them. She went back to her parents' house where Fleur was born and tried to start her life again without Pieter, but it was difficult. As she lay dying, she gave them to Fleur and told her they were the most precious gift she could give her and to wear them always. She closed her eyes for the last time and could feel his arms around her and almost believed in the joy.

CHAPTER 3

The night before Pieter had approached Vermeer about the portrait, he had put two and two together. He was inside his carriage on the way home from the tavern when the full realization came to him like a prophecy come true. The Mechelen had not been crowded and he had an opportunity to view the girl in detail. When she brought him his favorite ale he could not believe his eyes. He felt a shiver as if he were naked on the coldest night as he saw the earrings swinging happily beneath her turban. Vermeer's mother, Digna, had all of the girls wear them. But none adorned their turbans like Fleur's. His heart pounded like that of a raging bull. His face became hot and he feared his companions might sense his alarm. Pieter called to Digna and inquired about the new tavern maid, trying to remain calm, hoping she would not become suspicious. She went on to explain that Fleur was her friend Tessa's daughter. When she became ill from a weak heart malady Digna promised to care for her daughter if need be. When he questioned her about the father, her face turned to stone. She was quiet momentarily, and then claimed he had been killed in the Delft Thunderclap.

Pieter wanted to ride all night, never to return to his townhouse. His wife could wonder. If she was lonely it did not affect him. He loathed her company. His head started to ache and his harbored thoughts began to taunt him once again. Mathematics did not lie in seventeenth century Holland. They added up like the weight of beer barrels at his local warehouses. The downpour was not comforting. It was raining cats and dogs in his head. When the carriage stopped he rapped on the roof yelling for the driver to return to the Mechelen. He needed another round of ale and a final look at Fleur to confirm what he already knew to be true.

When he entered the Inn it seemed such a comfortable establishment. It felt like his new-found home. Now that he had found Fleur he was planning on spending every free moment there. He just longed to be near her. The Inn was one of the largest in Delft. It was popular for its great variety of ales and the special pig roast cooked slowly and made with secret spices. All of Digna's girls wore white collared, brownish sienna dresses and strikingly colorful turbans. Digna had once told him the turbans were not only pretty, they were neat. The girls' hair would not end up in someone's ale or fare. The Dutch were very clean, and unlike other parts of Europe even the poor strived to be neat. But Pieter thought Fleur looked enchanting, wearing it like no other maid could. She had a special aristocratic quality. The turban enhanced her features exposing the truth of her heritage. Combined with the earrings, the proof of her paternity was apparent.

As he sat at his regular spot, he was ecstatic to see Fleur was still working and called to her. "Fleur come sit with me a moment. You should have a break. You've been working a long time today." Fleur was suddenly struck shy and could not think of a reply. Pieter was determined to speak with her. "I will not kidnap you, I swear. Just have a word with me." Fleur sat gingerly next to Pieter and her face felt flushed or pale, of which, she was not sure. Pieter could feel his blood run in her veins. It took all of his meager strength not to shout out the truth. Fleur's large eyes were cast down, but he could see the beauty of her face and some of Tessa in her. She finally replied nervously, "It is quite cold today, sir, pray tell you have dressed warmly." Pieter's gaze seemed quite peculiar. None of the other men took such an interest. Usually they were most interested in peeking down her dress or making her hurry to fetch their next drink. Pieter obviously did not want her to leave and continued talking. "Oh Fleur you seem such a kind girl. I am so glad you are working here, brightening up the place with your youth." Fleur was flustered and momentarily at a loss for words. "Thank you sir, I enjoy helping Digna. She was good to take me in when Mother passed away." With these words her eyes teared up a bit and Pieter could not help putting his arm about her. "There, there my child, it must be a terrible thing to lose someone like Tessa." Fleur was shocked. How could someone from his circle have known her mother's name? She let the moment pass, and sat in silence, for his nearness felt good, right and wonderful.

Suddenly she excused herself, insisting she had to get back to her duties. Gracefully, she disembarked from Pieter's little embrace. He was sad to see her go. "Well my dear, do not fear. We all will take good care of you, I swear." Fleur was flabbergasted at his concern and thankful at the same time. "Thank you sir, you are also kind." As she hurried away the earrings did a dance that would enchant any man and Pieter felt at least a morsel of satisfaction. But it had never been more difficult to return home to Maria, the wife who had caused him to lose everything.

CHAPTER 4

The Mechelen was noisy and damp, yet Fleur moved like a warm watercolor. As Vermeer tried to avoid the crowd she appeared suddenly like the morning light. "Sir, you have come back. May I serve you wine or ale?" She brushed past him, a delicate butterfly, and his voice was the net that would capture her. Escaping foul breath and brew of local gossip he spirited her into the kitchen. Cook had gone home long ago, but he could still enjoy the smell of her special dishes that the Inn was famous for. Taking his cloak she thought it felt like Vermeer, a bit rough on the outside, but the inside fur was soft as his gaze, making her shiver. Without another word spent she knew he either wanted to paint her or make love to her. Vermeer was thinking how grateful he was to Pieter Van Ruijven. He was not only to be absolved of the debt; he was free to paint Fleur. She stood perfectly still, anxious for him to speak. He smiled and she suddenly felt relaxed and comfortable in his presence. "Fleur I need you to sit for me. I cannot pay you, but I will buy you some cloth and perhaps some paper for your funny little crafting. My mother has assured me you will remain employed at the Inn until you find your way or meet the man you will marry. I hope these things will not come to pass until I complete the portrait. My customer is very anxious to have a painting of a typical Dutch girl for his collection and will soon be moving to Rotterdam, so we must move quickly, but with excellence. Fleur did not know how to respond, but managed to reply, "But sir, where shall this take place?" Vermeer had worked this out with Mother earlier. "We will be clearing out the old storage room. I will be bringing my necessary tools here tomorrow. It is of the utmost urgency that we do not delay." Fleur could not completely digest all of the information that was being presented to her. Nor would she get a good night's sleep. But the artist went home and slept like a baby for the first time in months.

CHAPTER 5

The canals had frozen over fast. Vermeer hardly felt the change. His attention was focused on the center of his world. His inner eye explored every inch of the girl's face in many different ways. He would not start the painting officially until he had studied the subject in detail. He could see her emerging from the darkness. His palette was chosen, vermillion, yellow ochre, green earth, lead white, charcoal black and the exorbitantly expensive ultramarine. Thankfully, Pieter had supplied that as a great favor. Vermeer loved the idea of her in his mother's costume. With her hair tucked away in the turban she would appear more mysterious and alluring. He watched her face change at the Inn. Sometimes at dusk the sun would weave through the half closed shutters playing tricks on the angle of her cheekbones. She glowed in any light, emerging from the dark, a total angel brighter than any celestial body. When he picked up his brush and dipped it into the oil he thought of her moist skin. It was like a tulip blushing bright in the warm summer, just kissed good morning by the sun. But what amazed and enchanted him most were her lips. They exhibited the perfect combination of innocence and suggestion. He was ashamed to think of how he could brush his own lips lightly against hers. Suddenly he felt defeated and the force of the sin hit him square between the eyes. He was falling in love with Fleur. He could feel their bodies falling together like planets that would soon spin out of their orbit and crash. Vermeer had never transferred his passion from the canvas to any women of flesh. He devoured his models like so much candy without a thought or care for their human selves. He was too deeply involved in his craft and how he must adhere to the high standards of perspective, value, geometry and detail. The camera obscura, one of the earliest cameras, brought this to even greater heights. Yet he was about to throw away all of his ideals in order to complete this painting with time constraints. For her only would he abandon all of his beliefs, find new techniques? He would paint with full long strokes, fingers flying across the canvas taking form quickly, yet revealing every nuance. Pieter needed this completed in months, not years.

For the first time in weeks the temperature dropped below freezing. As he entered the Inn he saw Fleur was there as promised, wearing her turban and with eyes that no man could capture.

CHAPTER 6

The snow splashed white icy lace across the Dutch landscape like a crystal snowball. One tumble or shake and the world was awash with the splendor of winter. It lasted long and kept everyone cold for lengths of time. It's a wonder art flourished here in the European tundra, disguised with neat houses and maidens who looked more like daisies than twisted naked trees. Inside the citizens were tucked away with hot water bottles and pleasing fires.

The Vermeers and VanRuijvens do not travel in the same circles. Nonetheless, Pieter and Johannes are best friends. They enjoy dinner together occasionally, and Maria can be quite the hostess, laughing and discussing the latest trends in the art world with her guests. She has great respect for Vermeer and supports her husband's patronage. Owning breweries seems so unpolished yet there is an art to making the finest ale that is the talk of Holland. This love of art is the one thing they have in common. Her taste is impeccable. Over the years her astute purchases of great variety helped their already massive fortune grow. Occasionally he is sad he cannot love her. She never had a chance. Tessa haunted their marriage like the ghost in "Hamlet." The blood was always on his hands. He had murdered every chance for a successful marriage when he walked away from Tessa. Greed and misplaced obedience had tipped the scales in favor of this shallow relationship. Now his parents had passed on and he was stuck on this earth with Maria. She had tried so hard, he so little. They both loved their toy dogs and he enjoyed walking with them and his wife in the gardens. It took away some of the pain and gave them time to appear a normal couple. They visited a spa in Switzerland every year with their daughter, Magdalena. Why could he not feel? Would he always be numb? Would money continue to rule his existence to the end? He had heard of Tessa's death and wept for days, when he was alone in the quarters.

Maria was calling him to dinner now. She would look at him across the table with her too small eyes. Their grayness seemed to expose her soul. She would chatter for a while, hoping, hanging on for a response that was always delayed. If they were not discussing art, her subject matter was of little importance to him. But he was a kind man by nature, easy going. This was his nemeses, his nature. It is why he caved in to his parents' demands. But we are what we are born to be and he could see no end.

CHAPTER 7

Vermeer could not sleep. Thoughts were wearing him out, challenging his endurance. Nothing would better Fleur. She would wear her turban and tavern dress. More would be too much, less too little. Pieter wishes to remember her as he first saw her, no distractions, and no props. There would be no map, window, letter or lace. Of course, she would wear the earrings that Pieter had given Tessa all those years ago. To Vermeer the earrings were of little consequence compared to the radiance of her features. Their glimmer only served to make the onlooker gaze at her for one more moment as they swung back and forth continuing to mesmerize. They led you on like a lure does to the fish and when it is too late you are totally captivated. It is sinful the way he looks upon her. The bible quotes better he pluck out his eye. He should not covet her when he has such a loving wife waiting for him at the Papist corner, especially one who has carried his children for over half of their married life. He did love her, but he could not stop his feelings for Fleur. How ironic that he is being forced to paint the very subject he longs for. This is his chance to act upon his animal instinct. Most important, it is a legitimate excuse to relieve his debts, manhood and artist's inclination in one sweep of the brush. There could be no obstacles. He must move forward like the lion upon the lamb.

He awakened as if he had not slept and hurried in slow motion to his appointment. The cold should have helped him be aware of his surroundings, but he was far too deep in thought when he passed the Mechelen and needed to turn back. Pieter practically bumped into him as he opened the door and seemed happy to see him. Vermeer did not even greet him. "The painting is started in my mind, Pieter. It has come to me what will most please you. I will bring you to her sooner than the other paintings you have entrusted me to complete." Pieter's face changed suddenly, like a gray cloud passing over the sun. He looked troubled and began to brood. Pieter's reply was firm and he did not intend to be challenged. "Yes, that is excellent. However, I need to view it on a regular basis upon her absence. I realize this is highly irregular and deviates from your trade codes, but it is most necessary. I need some history, some insight into this subject." They entered the Inn and left the blustery wind behind that was pushing the clouds faster now imitating their own urgency.

CHAPTER 8

Catarina, to this day, could not believe her mother had not blocked her marriage to Vermeer, because he was Protestant. Protestants and Catholics were like oil and water, in Delft. The papist corner where they lived teemed only with devout Catholics. Johannes had converted in order to please his mother-in-law, since then, Vermeer had been accepted as master of the Guild of St. Luke's. His talent was apparent and he rose. Unfortunately, his talent did not keep up with their financial needs.

She was a plainly pretty girl, with fair skin, high brow and straight nose. Her eyes were small and dark in contrast to her blond ringlets. The love they shared was not a torrent. It started out like a sunny, drizzly day. The years crisscrossed like the town's canals. Eleven children brought them together and created a silent distance, all at once. At night he could be tender. The warmth under the down quilt helped them enjoy their lovemaking and hatched one duckling after another. It was an endless journey. Her body was the road and giving birth happened at every rest stop along the way. He always said pregnancy enhanced her beauty. Against all the Dutch masters' rules he painted her twice with child, finding her aesthetic in full bloom. He was wonderful when she posed for him, holding a letter.

He told her she was his muse, his good wife. She loved when he said that her greatest art were all of her children, and the gentle manner with which she mothered them. They are all sculptures, each unique. When he painted her, she was happiest, even more so than when they made love. She knew that painting her brought their relationship full circle, from the drudgery of everyday life, to what she knew was his greatest pleasure.

CHAPTER 9

It was a great coincidence, Vermeer thought, that since he had laid his eyes on Fleur he was drawn to her and now he would paint her. It was not such beauty alone. It laid somewhere inside like a hidden treasure sunk deep in the bluest waters of the new world. He wanted to explore and discover all of her natural resources. What perfect timing. Pieter was making his wish come true. He would sail for the land of Fleur and bring back her bounty for his patron. But how will they keep this secret in a town like Delft. For now, his mother had not been properly informed, not wanting her involved. However, she was a shrewd woman and eventually would be privy to all. Thankfully, Reynier, his father, had demanded self control and taught the family honor, and keeping confidences was part of it. His mother was hard and kind at the same time. You had to chisel away at her for a while until she was ready to let go and warm up your heart with hers. She had agreed to lend him the old storage room, if it helped feed her grandchildren. Fleur, as a typical Dutch girl, would be perfect. His customer would be pleased for she found the girl pleasing to look upon. Her goodness and wholesome qualities would help place a higher value on the piece.

The deal was struck, all was settled. He was painting away. His household was just thinking he needs two studios to get money in the door. But still he was not fully recovered from the triple shock; she was Pieter's daughter from Tessa, he would have a legitimate excuse to paint her, and he would soon be free of the Van Ruijven debt. He felt high like on a wizard's drug. He came to earth when he realized he had to find a way to work on his other orders as well. There needs to be guilders to support his family that multiplied like spring bulbs. Thin air and warm water could sustain him, but he had no right to make his household suffer. He loved even his mother-in-law. Yet, this was something that caused him no guilt. It was like inhabiting another planet with different laws and morals. Nothing seemed alien about his feelings and behavior. He had acquired a new set of values that lined up with his desires. It seemed perfectly normal to envision Fleur with him lying by the canal under a shady tree. The bees knew to stay away and the birds knew to sing for them. He was ecstatic and full of youthful curiosity, like the old man layer he had grown was peeling off fifteen years. He wanted to know every nook and cranny of her lush body, visit her rain forest and lie in her valley with no shame.

He realized his wife Catarina would have to be aware of the situation on some level. But she will never be told the whole truth regarding the fact that Fleur is Pieter's daughter. More importantly, she must never know his inappropriate feelings for Fleur; he would never hurt her so. Luckily, she did not pry into his affairs. Whatever he told her she would simply be relieved to be free of the Van Ruijven clutch, no matter how soft the gloves.

He was almost home now. He knew the

children's activities would soon drain him of his carnal thoughts. So he looked at Fleur one last time, wide eyes and full soft lips. She was a willow tree and her skin was like the softest petals. He had touched her arms and hands at the Inn and knew this to be true. But how could you ever escape the shape of her face and curve of her neck? How would he interpret this to the world? It was a great responsibility. He kissed her goodnight and the velvet of her tongue aroused him. Perhaps this was all a dream and he would wake up to an empty canvas and relentless debt that would be the death of him.

CHAPTER 10

Vermeer thought he would paint the vision that he first gazed upon. He had come to the Mechelen as a refuge from the ruckus of the children. His neck ached from a long day spent laboring in his studio and he found no comfort at home. As he entered the establishment Fleur was the first person he saw. Like a fox that had just scented her prey she turned and looked at him. The first glimpse of her was the line of her cheek and impossible eyes, opened wide revealing her free spirit. A mix of curiosity and intrigue, he was drawn to her with the instincts of a lion. Yes, this is how he would paint her.

Now she was here before him and was his model. This was freedom to take a subject and go where your talent took you. Yes, that was the pose. There was no question. He seated her to his liking and he asked she gently turn her face towards him. From there it was like the unraveling of colorful ribbon.

He had completed the basics, applying loosely granulated layers. The four main stages were done. The lighting scheme had finally been worked out. The under painting stage complete, he sat in front of his easel, small palette in hand. He was constantly struggling for artistic expression. He sought natural illumination and was determined Fleur would shine like an immortal, mythical goddess of beauty. For the balance of their time together, he would stand so he could walk back and forth envisioning the totality of his work. The soul of the painting was laid down. Now comes the flesh and blood. For without a good foundation there would be no depth. Objects would collapse upon themselves. Faces would be flat like those found in the paintings of medieval times. That is why they were called the dark ages. He wanted to bring his works to imitate life, so five hundred years from now his generation would be remembered in detail. The future of his work emanated from the first, most important strokes.

He felt the labor of this painting. It would be like giving birth to Fleur. This is why Pieter insisted on seeing it at every stage. He was trying to recapture her entire life. He did not wish to miss a morsel. He had created her, but Vermeer also would have a hand in this. He would command the color of her eyes, the tint of her soft skin. These combined with the coolness of blues and warmth of sienna would give birth to his final work. The labor would be great. Exhaustion was a drug that he could not rehabilitate himself from. Usually, he drove himself for two years on one painting. Detail would be his death. But this could not be. He had a six-month deadline. Pieter could be so cruel. When the flowers were waking up he must be ready to present the child. He could make it happen, but he would somehow continue in excellence. He loved the smell of the oil and paint and the feel of the brush in his hand. For hours he could work and forget to eat or relieve himself. Work mixed with nothing. Art was work and work was his life. He forgot he had children and could be a bachelor for all he cared as he glided across the canvas. Only this was important, the moment when he dipped his thirsty bristles in the flame of red and the most precious bone white. The colors brought form giving birth to his final work. Each moment was thought out and measured.

Finally he stopped his pondering. She was sitting quietly waiting for him to begin. "Turn your face towards me, slightly. Turn to the right. Your chin, keep it down a bit and look up." She loved to listen to his voice. It mesmerized her and she felt it would be possible to sit here for eternity. She could stare at him for hours and respond to his every command. It gave her a valid excuse to be near him. If it meant living with a stiff neck, she had no care. Each day she was consumed by the thought of how she could please him without moving. She had never traveled so far without motion. He had opened up her mind and she felt worldly and years older. She never thought of the things that he prodded her to. Instead Vermeer was the love that would burn in her mind. For him she would place her tongue just so. Her eyes would dance and light up for the man before her, not some young fool. He was her inspiration. For a painter he seemed quite blind, for her passion for him was as plain as the smile on Da Vinci's Mona Lisa. Those dangerous thoughts would keep her busy that winter, while across the room Vermeer deflected them like poisonous arrows.

CHAPTER 11

Catarina had gone through her trunk and favorite possessions. She would approach Maria this afternoon before the dinner they were invited to this evening. The debt was gnawing away at her like an embryo that needed too much nutrition. Nothing would make her happier than helping her artist husband rise in society. If she could get the debt reduced he would be pleased and it would benefit their marriage as well. There were several pieces of Delft porcelain that Mrs. Van Ruijven would love to add to her collection. The windmill was especially exquisite. The workmanship was lovely with its traditional blue and white colors. Carefully she packed up her precious cargo and hurried towards the Van Ruijven home in the Protestant section of Delft.

The door of the Van Ruijven home was alone daunting. The knocker was heavy gold and must be worth more than her trousseau, and her family was far from poor. A young buxom girl with snowflake colored braids led her to a room where the hearth was glowing and warmth emanated through, leaving the cold winter behind for others to worry about. Maria, who was a difficult woman to read, seemed to be in a good mood. "Catarina welcome, I was not expecting you until this evening." Catarina replied with deference, "Oh forgive me. I am so sorry to surprise you like this. I hope you will be glad when you see what I am offering." Maria smiled, which was rare, and Catarina thought if she did this more often it would help her homely looks. "Just sit down dear and the maid will bring us hot cocoa. It is imported from Switzerland and wonderfully delicious. I appreciate the company, Pieter just returned from The Hague. Business kept him away for several weeks. His return yesterday was a great relief. I have been very lonely." The fire crackled and the light danced around the room. Catarina never tired of this house and of its pleasures. "I see you continue to decorate your private room with Vermeer's paintings. We are very grateful for your patronage." Maria continued to smile. "Yes, I enjoy the details and his style. He is the greatest painter in all of Holland, I assure you. History will someday prove me right. How quaint that he painted you with child in the portrait where you hold a letter. If only my husband adored me so." Catarina parceled out her reply with great tact and caution. "I am sure he loves you truly. Look at all the gifts he bestows upon you." She motioned her delicate hand around the room. Maria's face darkened and Catarina tried to change the subject by offering up the contents of the box. Maria's face did not indicate her inner delight. Catarina went on, "I know my husband is in your debt and I would like to help reduce it in my own way." Maria took each piece and with the expert eye of a critic, took time to examine every detail. "I see you are aware of my Delft Porcelain collection. I am always looking to expand, but with only the finest pieces. Therefore, I am only interested in the shoe and especially the windmill. I am going to offer you a high price for the windmill because I have been searching for one just like it." Quickly they negotiated a fair amount for the pieces Maria had selected. With both disappointment and elation Catarina negotiated a fair settlement. Maria had been generous and the deduction would be substantial. The women finished their cocoa, talking more of the evening's impending dinners, which both were looking forward to.

They finished their visit and Catarina was relieved to depart. She was glad the debt was reduced, but sadly, Maria did not accept the entire collection.

CHAPTER 12

The dinner was quite delicious. Maria sat silently through most of the evening. She did comment on the porcelain shoe and had it displayed in the parlor room. Pieter had been informed of the purchase and assured Maria he would subtract the value from the debt. He thought to himself what a waste it had been for Johannes. The debt would soon enough be erased without the porcelain sale. But it was good for Catarina to believe she had helped her husband rise above their circumstances in her own way. Maria looked sour to him. Her face was drawn and he found it difficult to make eye contact with her. She could be a gracious hostess and she did chat with Vermeer about a few of the many works they owned. He was very patient, answering all her questions while his dutiful wife remained in the background with little to say. He liked Catarina. She was a pleasant girl with a good word about everyone.

He was suddenly impatient to whisk Vermeer off to his library to discuss their business. The women could drink cordials and warm themselves by the fire the maid was efficiently stoking. As they walked down the impressive hallways, Johannes was studying some of the tapestries. They seemed more interesting to him than the paintings tonight. Tapestry and beer were two of the biggest exports for Delft and Pieter had the best of both. His breweries were the largest in Holland and his tapestry collection the most famous. As they entered the library, Johannes was momentarily envious. The books stood side by side in great numbers ranging from Cicero to modern day writers. The intricately carved desk and bookcases glowed against the numerous candles that the servants lit each night so their master could read if he chose. The smell of polish and leather were gentle and provoked one to think only intellectual thoughts and long to sit and read endlessly, as Pieter often did. Vermeer knew that under the boyish exterior was a highly intelligent and complex man, one that he greatly respected and relied upon. How fortunate that he was his friend. "Tonight, Vermeer, we strike the final deal. I will have the papers drawn up at my lawyer's office. It will eliminate the balance due in a legal fashion. However, it will not become binding until I have seen it and am satisfied with the final portrait of Fleur." Johannes who always thought before he spoke sat enjoying the manliness of the room. It enveloped him providing the inspiration needed to seal the negotiations and bring this matter to an agreeable end. "Pieter, I have already finished the work in my mind. I am certain you will be more than satisfied. Fleur will be as easy to paint as the prettiest tulips along the Delft canals. I will not only show you her outside, but her spirit will be reflected as well. I hope this adventure will seal our friendship which is already strong for it means much to both me and Catarina." Pieter was looking very comfortable and handsome in his favorite chair and expensive silk stockings. For the first time in weeks he seemed at ease. Vermeer suddenly looked worried. "And your wife, how shall you explain all of this?" Pieter waited to respond until he lit his favorite cigar. "You need not concern yourself. She is free to purchase all her trinkets. I have never pulled in the financial reins on her. She needs no explanation in this matter. This will repay me for all of the pettiness and needling I have endured for seventeen years and for the loss of the love that you will help bring back to me.

CHAPTER 13

The spires of Delft reminded Pieter's wife, Maria, of huge weapons. Her temperament today was sharp. She felt as if she had performed self mutilation with them. Pieter was gone far too often. His guild meetings were excessive. He worked late at the brewery for the first time in years, claiming the competition was catching up with him. This she did not believe for an instant. She had an astute business head and would have excelled had she been born male. She kept an eye on all the markets and values important in the trading world. She could read and write and do sums faster than Lloyds of London, but could not reconcile her failing marriage. Loneliness was deeper than a well, and when she peered into it, blackness had no end. Why could he not rest by the fire at night with his feet propped upon his expensive Moroccan hassock? She would have the servant retrieve his favorite book of poetry from the library or perhaps she would read him Cicero or Homer.

What was keeping him so occupied? Although they slept in separate bedrooms she heard him creeping around late in the evening. She sat up in her canopy bed with the surrounding lace wide open so she could hear everything. Needing little sleep, her calculating mind worked around the clock. Her plan was hatching and she expected results. If only she had conceived a male heir. Magdalena, their daughter, had little effect on Pieter. She was a spoiled child and their relationship revolved around material things. Still, she was musically talented and the highest achiever in academics. He did praise her from time to time, but his heart was elsewhere. Her little King Charles beagles were her only comfort. Imported from England, they were bred for only the wealthiest of Europe. Each night they snuggled with her completely unaware of her unpopularity. They adored her. They did not care a fig about their pedigree or hers.

Her worst enemy was her mirror that showed a face lacking not only beauty, but youth as well. Some henna here, a little powder there, were found of little use. Her expensive crèmes assuaged her temporarily. They helped her masquerade, covering up the gashes and lines that sorrow etched on a face which could endure no more.

CHAPTER 14

Maria had her servants' rooms searched by the head housekeeper, randomly. This was, of course, unbeknownst to the help. Nothing got by her sharp eye. She was intelligent, resourceful and self serving. She held the porcelain windmill that she planted in Gertrude's bedroom and felt great purpose in what she planned. This windmill would blow her worries away and Gertrude would be the hand to deal it, if she did not wish to go to jail.

Why was Pieter at the Inn so often these past months? She had to know the truth. He was using the guild and brewery as his excuse to be away. But there was something amiss and she would find out. Several hours later, Gertrude stood before her quivering in her clogs. Maria's face was as hard as the lion knocker. "Well Gertrude, what do you have to say for yourself?" She had the little windmill sitting innocently on her end table. Gertrude was very confused and began to cry. Maria offered no comforting words. "It is clear you have stolen this from me. You will regret your action. I will give you two choices: the police, or do something for me, exactly as I direct you." The fire crackled behind them, dancing and taunting Gertrude. She wanted to jump into it like a big log and disappear into the cold night. But there was no escape from the fiery eyes of her mistress.

Gertrude made a futile attempt to deny her

involvement in such a deed. Her mind was racing. How and why could this have happened? Who would put her in such a terrible predicament? Maria had no pity. "I am sending you to the Mechelen to work for Vermeer's mother. You will report to me weekly. I want to know every move my husband makes, who he speaks to, who he looks at, when he leaves and most importantly what he says. Do not fail me or I will fail you. Now pack your things." Gertrude was a pretty girl, round and lusty. She had blue eyes that men could swim in, and pure white hair. She used all of her assets to her advantage and now her life depended on them. She was a simple girl who could not read or write. She was poor and after living in such an opulent home, she longed to be rich.

Life was unfair. She should be Mrs. Van Ruijven, but she would hate to look like her. How her husband would love to have a beautiful woman. Maria was homely and skinny and she knew Pieter did not love her. It was the way he did not look at her. There was never any touching or intimacy between them. He never snuck into her bed in the middle of the night, as married couples do. She wondered how he had been forced into such a wretched marriage. Well, that was none of her business, but it would be her business to complete this mission. What could Maria be after? Anyway, it will be interesting to observe Mr. Van Ruijven away from the constraints of this house.

CHAPTER 15

Before ensnaring Gertrude, Maria had gone to Digna, Vermeer's mother and explained she needed a favor. Her servants were tripping over each other and she needed to release Gertrude. She would give a set amount of guilders for Digna to take her in. She would also bestow upon her a porcelain windmill that she could add to her own collection. Gertrude was a good girl who had potential to be an excellent tavern maid. She was hard working and minded her own business. As she said this, she knew it was completely untrue. Gertrude was actually very sloppy and often tripped over her own two feet. She knew she was sly and this was all that mattered. Digna knew she could not deny her. Maria's family had been her son's patron for years. They had purchased so much of his art and he was in great debt to them as well.

Digna was momentarily at a loss for words, but soon composed herself. She smiled and Maria was immediately jealous of her fading beauty. "Oh Maria, I have just one trundle bed left in the attic. She can share the room with Fleur." Maria thought how perfect this little scenario could be. Digna continued, "They are close in age and they will be good company for each other. The Inn has been extremely busy and I was thinking of getting another hand. You have solved another problem for me. There are lots of beds to make as well as beer mugs to fill. She will have a multitude of tasks." Maria was ecstatic. "She is not very bright, but she does know how to put in a good day's work. I think you will find you will profit from her best in the tavern. Men will certainly want her to cater to them, so they can have a little flirtation with their spirits. I truly believe this will benefit your purse and make your customers happy to return to the Mechelen. Meanwhile, I will have a manageable household. I assure you all will be well and both our lives will become a little easier. It is time you took some leisure Digna, you are not getting any younger.

CHAPTER 16

Gertrude stared at the walls. Her fate was met. The mistress had planted the windmill and her innocence would never be proven. She was almost finished packing when the housekeeper's voice came ringing louder than the church bells. "Gertrude the Mechelen has sent the cart. Move this very moment or you will go without your scanty belongings." Gertrude answered her instantly "I am hurrying along Ma'm. You can be certain I am taking my leave as fast as I can." She was not a feisty girl, just one that could keep a secret and watch out for her own back. She stumbled with her bundle half -opened and scarves sticking out, not looking tidy at all. It was a long trip from the servants' quarters to the outside. Finally, after almost tripping down the steps and bumping into the scullery maid, she was in sight of her ride. In a way she was glad to escape her fate here. Mrs. Van Rijuen was very strict. Every moment was spent catering to her smallest whim. Sometimes she just wanted to scream and slap the woman right in the face and laugh about it, without a care to the poverty that would be waiting for her without her job. Her mother had run off with the footman leaving her behind. This is possibly why Maria had chosen her for this rotten job. She thought perhaps the mistress would have taken pity upon her and at least let her keep her position. How foolish and naive she had been. The only pleasure had been the treats she snuck up to her closet that was called a room. Plus she loved looking at Maria's husband. He was like a prince charming, the most dashing master in all of Delft. She just knew he thought she was pretty and wished he could sneak her into his oversized bed. They would close the curtains and Maria would be none the wiser.

Once outside, the cold ripped though her thin shawl with no mercy. She looked back one last time. There stood Maria behind the largest middle window, the gargoyles surrounding her, a grotesque frame. She looked like the head witch of the household, but Gertrude knew for certain she had never picked up a broom.

The canals rushed by buildings with their spires and towers pointed to the sky in the distance, which seemed to be her only escape. The carriage wheels made soft noises above the snow and the driver seemed in no hurry to return to work. Last night's storm had been cleaned up and the street was lined with clusters of snow piles that were laid out in the orderly fashion of the Dutch. The sky looked grey and angry like a Roman soldier's shield in battle. Suddenly the sky shifted slightly and a warm ray blessed Gertrude's forehead like a benediction, providing a moment's peace. The future loomed before her like a dragon ready to eat the damsel in distress.

CHAPTER 17

The painting was taking shape and form, but until complete he did not want Fleur to look upon it. Today she was cleaning the storage room when he entered. She heard the squeaky door and felt his presence like the rapture, making her stomach flutter. His dark eyes and fuzzy long hair seemed not to match his other traits. He moved smoothly and with a kind of confidence. Yet, there was heaviness about him like he was always thinking or off somewhere else. She could not wait to converse with him for it fed her these days. "Hello Vermeer, I am still amazed that you are actually painting my portrait for the entire world to see. That is what I have been thinking over." Vermeer looked surprised at her remark. "Well now, Fleur, I have one patron who will surely look upon it, but I do not think he will show it to the world. He likes to hide my works in his house in great numbers and not one has yet escaped. However, you may have a point. Unlike us, art lives on and changes hands over the centuries. Some like 'The Three Graces' have been reworked since the time of ancient Greece to reflect the era. Your portrait may be passed down until no one remembers my patron was in ownership." Fleur looked intrigued. "Yes, I thought of that, and also if I would die without my image left behind, in one hundred years it would be like I never existed. Now in a sense I will live on. That is an important aspect of art. It allows future generations to understand how people lived and looked in the past." The man stood in front of her and became introspective.

He could not imagine a world without his golden angel so he quickly changed the subject. "Let me make a fire and warm ourselves so we may work in comfort. There is much to complete today. I expect to work until last light."

As he gathered the logs he fell silent. The kindling hissed and whispered the truth. The couple watched it glow and bring further romance into the setting. Fleur glanced at him as she continued wiping the table and mopping the cracked floor. She scrubbed the windows with all of her might so the sun would fully assist the master. The girl was brought out of her daydream. "Now Fleur I need you to sit. Think of beautiful things or a boy you may love. Keep that mystery about you. It will make the spectator work at understanding you. They will bring their young sons, soon to be men, and say this is a woman. This is the face that will bring you to manhood." Fleur was suddenly afraid. Vermeer stopped in his tracks and turned his attention to arranging his palette. Fleur could not look at him or her countenance would be a dead giveaway. She excused herself momentarily or she would surely wet her simple petticoat. His voice had great power over her anatomy and she could no longer control her heart or other delicate matters.

CHAPTER 18

There were two floors to serve. The Mechelen boasted an unprecedented number of tables and rustic ambience that all members of Delft society longed to enjoy. Downstairs the long bar and barrel-like tables were home to the fish monger, butcher and other men with small stands in the square. They were from the poorer class, but none-the-less they were content with their lot. They drank beer that sometimes led to loud singing which Digna rarely tolerated. Of course, the more homely girls waited on them. But the men still enjoyed pinching their backsides now and again. Digna was an astute business woman who reserved the privacy of the upper level for wealthy businessmen, tradesmen and merchants. Here they were pampered by young tavern maids with bright eyes and saucy smiles. They carried their trays full of the finest ales, aperitifs and oxen stew. Digna excelled at keeping the growing bourgeois class drunk and their stomachs full of delicacies. These men kept their hands to themselves. They were not gruff and kept their lustier thoughts tucked under their fine woolen caps, though the girls could feel them staring at their tender places as they hurried to fill pitchers and fetch wine. The Mechelen was always in good spirits. Everyone had fun, but there were no brawls or excessive foul language. Johannes was a good son helping when he could, jumping behind the bar when it was busy or fixing a broken stool. Digna and Johannes were not affectionate outwardly, but warmth emanated between them and they worked as a team which helped relieve both their burdens.

Fleur was working upstairs as usual. Digna would not allow her to set foot elsewhere. This is where another man presently spent more time than Vermeer. His name was Pieter Van Ruijven. Apparently he was consumed with the Guild of St Luke's affairs. He also had a thriving brewery business that he seemed to run from the Inn these days. What was it that drew him to her? He had fine patrician features. A well-kept mustache was topped with an aquiline nose. His eyes looked familiar, golden brown with lashes any Dutch girl would envy. His graying temples did little to distract. They made him all the more handsome. His thick, dark hair fell over his shoulders in the style of the day and his garments were the height of fashion. They had several conversations, but often Fleur would see him watching her silently from a distance with the kindest eyes she had ever seen. They lingered on her and she could almost read his thoughts. He was a gentle and patient man who hated to argue over politics or anything for that matter. Obviously he was an important citizen and natural leader. Most men deferred to him, so he could afford to be soft spoken instead of crass. It seemed the loudest ruffians were the ones who had trouble getting the attention. The new girl, Gertrude, was getting lots of attention too. She was going out of her way to show off an ankle or bend over a table a little longer than necessary. This behavior was earning her a few extra tips that the men were happy to pay. Pieter's wife had sent her away to work here and help Digna. Vermeer had told her in confidence that they had an abundance of servants and her mother had run off with the footman. Maria did not want the responsibility of a young girl. Digna wanted to help because of their tolerance of his debt, and in reality she really needed the help. His mother was looking tired and older so he felt it worked well for all parties. Fleur was glad to have the new girl's company. Suddenly she felt a customer brush past and touch her breasts as he grabbed his wine. It happened so fast she would have trouble convincing a witness it happened, especially since she was on the upper floor.

CHAPTER 19

Vermeer was taking one last look. Today would be about thought and study, angles, turns and curves. He had to get his artist's house in order. What color are those eyes exactly? How would it feel to paint her lower lip? Could it be duplicated? He was not God, but, he was certain he could.

The storage room was empty except for a cot, table and artists' tools. He was being parsimonious in every material aspect because he was resolving a debt. He should be happy he was not spending too much time and money. What he would spend at the rate of a dog race addict placing bets, would be his ultimate genius and meted out in a most economical fashion. It would be the design of little nothing but one subject. His greatest work would be most sublime. Uncluttered, everything left to the eyes and mind that studied it. There would be little help in moving the imagination forward. Time was of the essence. He would orchestrate the oil and paint across the canvass of time that would never end until his debt to Pieter was erased. He hated that art and money blended together like gold leaf and sewage, but there was nothing he could do. Extraneous articles would not exist in this painting. The viewer must do some of the work, but it would be the kind you could immerse yourself in and at the end of the day, love your job more than being home by the fire.

Fleur could not understand Vermeer at all. He

was secretive and kind, crabby and at times funny. As he worked he would try to cheer her up in an effort to provide a relaxed atmosphere. "Fleur, you look like you are sucking on the pickle meister's thumb. Fleur, the butcher will not cut you up for market tonight, I promise." Just when her neck was about to break, he would lighten her spirits getting another hour out of her. It was just the beginning, and if it meant a broken neck, she would be glad for the sacrifice. She actually would not care if he slowed down to a halt. She could look at him for a long time and never forget him, when he picked up his hat and disappeared into the Delft mist late at night when his eyes were ready for bed.

CHAPTER 20

With the Spanish War behind them the Netherlands was emerging as a nation to be contended with. The bourgeois class was growing rapidly. There was a great variety of industry, tapestries, breweries, Delft tile and Delft porcelain. All were busily moving along the road of fortune. Of course, there were poor people giving those on top a view of the bottom, so they could further enjoy their good fortune. It was a historical necessity. What is poor? Well, in Delft, in the mid-1660's, it was a combination of people and trades perfuming this rising class of newcomers and trying in their own way to imitate them. And art was the greatest imitator. It was peaking at this time. The poorest man had a carving of some lowly type, while the rich man's painting might be worth the price of a spacious, Dutch home. Art rises to the top, but there was a strong trickle effect in seventeenth century Holland. It boasted more artists than in all of France, a larger and more historically cultured country. But the Dutch people loved objects and form. It was a national pastime to appreciate their environment. Hence, art blossomed and became an important part of the people.

In those hundred years, literally millions of paintings were painted, bought and sold, of which today, less than one percent exist. Most Dutch masters sold their paintings far and wide, increasing their fame and fortune.

Unfortunately, Vermeer did the opposite. He had few patrons, mainly in Delft, who monopolized his output. But of course, Vermeer could not have known that by selling to the chosen few he was doing a disservice to his immediate future. Had he expanded his marketing horizons he may have lived past middle age. Unfortunately, the mechanisms that drove him were tightly linked to the mouths of his wife and eleven children. He could not think past his next commission that was right around the papist corner. He plodded ahead tediously working his art with precision, repositioning, reworking, redoing, sometimes with the added benefit of the camera obscura.

If only he did not have to concern himself with finances. He would paint only for the sake of art, wearing the same clothing, eating like a monk from the strictest order. It was the Dutch Golden Age and his art would emerge like the sun. The vow of silence would be welcome. However, he could not live without the touch of a woman. His sexual appetite did not abate with age or exhaustion from the effort of his work. He prayed every Sunday at mass with great fervor in hopes Christ would show him the way to salvation, for damnation was now almost certain. As a former Protestant he could never agree with Catholics' obsession with iconic status, but now he looked the sacred heart right in the eye as he begged forgiveness. Now to compound matters his needs have grown to monstrous proportions. The two-headed beast taunts him of the slaughter that will soon take place if he does not control his libido. Yet, he was not a deeply religious man. When he sought out the Lord he felt abandoned and was more fulfilled by secular matters. These were his thoughts as he entered the Guild of St. Luke's meeting leaving behind his fears and sins for the dragon to devour.

CHAPTER 21

William has brought him to his boiling point once again. Lazy and corpulent, he is the opposite of Catarina. It is despicable the way he visits his home when he wants an advance from his mother. Vermeer has great respect for his mother-in-law on many counts. She is one of his greatest benefactors believing in his genius, supporting him at times so he can complete an assignment that drags on because he cannot compromise. She tries to push him to work faster, but to no avail and she is never angry with him. She knows he is a virtual workhorse, painting day in and out as he chips away at his debt. The problem with his brother-in-law William is that he rarely works and gambles his and her money away. He is her only son and she cannot turn him away. Watching her assist him to further his misery is painful for his wife, Catarina. He has to leave the house when he sees William. He cannot deal with this. It is so depressing it could affect his ability to paint. Catarina says nothing as he gathers his cloak, but gives him a look like he is abandoning her once again, leaving her to deal with her slovenly brother.

The weather is getting colder. The canals are freezing over and it is getting harder to keep the house warm. His studio is frigid, but his hand keeps moving. If it gets too cold he grinds paint and cleans his brushes letting himself fall into the pattern of an artist's life. But William has dashed all hopes of him painting anything more today. He will go to the Mechelen and gaze upon

Fleur. The canvas of his mind will compare her to the final stages he has come to in his quest to reproduce her utter loveliness. Suddenly he is filled with guilt. He is thinking of her naked. If only he could rid her of clothing and paint the flesh he so longs to touch and know like a man instead of an artist. He brings his hand to his heart, the one that should be beating for Catarina. How can he feel this way? His wife has given him everything his mother never could. This is why his love is more maternal than lustful. Her softness surrounds him often. He enjoys entering her lovely vessel. She satisfies his needs without hesitation, and reaches out to him in the night. Yet, something has always been missing and now the blow has been dealt. When he first saw Fleur it was like The Delft Thunderclap when much of the town was destroyed by great quantities of gunpowder which exploded. The Mechelen and all of Pieter's breweries had been spared. His insides burned for her like the fire that was its aftermath. She is the Helen of Troy he longed for as a young man. Homer could not have known such beauty. Could Helen have compared? This is how the Trojan felt when he sailed away with his prize. The animal in him was clawing its way out. He had to whip it and beat it back, calming himself before he went into the Inn. Catarina, I do love you, you have inspired me to live day to day and paint to provide for our brood. But Fleur you are the masterpiece.

CHAPTER 22

Fleur opened the attic door and the winter bit her right in the face. The hot water bottle in her bed had gone cold hours ago and the chill was intense. But she still needed to inhale her fresh air each morning and stretch like a flower reaching for the sun. It had been a ritual. Her mother did this each day until she was so sick she could not rise from her bed. Gertrude was sleeping, lightly snoring. Her ringlets hung around the pillow like gentle ripples in the town's canals. She was a pretty thing, feminine yet big and strong. She never met anyone who asked so many questions. It was good to have a friend. Now that her mother was gone she had lost her only one. She was always so busy helping her mother with the flower stand and learning paper art. There was never a need for anyone else in her life. How foolish she was to think that could go on forever.

Her mother had spent so much time with her teaching Fleur everything she knew. Tessa's parents had once been fairly affluent traders until the collapse of the local market during the war with Spain. Therefore, as a girl she had learned to read and write. Although she was consumed with supporting them she made sure her daughter learned the basics. Fleur was very bright and learned quickly. She was also talented and thrived when she worked on her paper art. At a young age she invented new designs for animals and flowers. At the Inn she had a chance to sell some of her work to the customers to bring home to their wives as gifts. With this money she could buy some cloth and small necessities.

She worked long hours at the Inn but the work was not heavy. Her feet did ache at night and when she slept she was too tired to dream. But when she did it was always about him painting her portrait. It was almost finished and when he applied the last stroke she woke up. She could not understand why he had chosen her to model. Gertrude seemed more beautiful and full bodied. She had large hips and breasts that spilled over her dress like the foam of an overfilled glass of ale.

Fleur was very anxious to see the completed painting. It was the most exciting thing that ever happened to her. She felt like the heroine of a romance novel. She took out the precious diary her mother had given her for her fourteenth birthday. She made sure she wrote down the most important events of each day. Today she would write one word, "Johannes."

CHAPTER 23

"Fleur, come and fill me up, but pray speak to me a bit." Fleur came hurrying across the glossy floor with little effort. She was light on her feet and did all tasks and movements with the finesse of a dancer. "Sir, but I do not know what to say. My conversation may not be to your liking. I know little of what is going on in the world for I have been quite busy. Perhaps it would be in my favor to do so and learn more of what is occurring around me." Pieter could feel the strength of her sweetness as she came near. She was like a parfait layered in good things. He struggled to relax and forget his anxiety. "Tell me about your family and why you are not with them." His eyes flickered ever so slightly and his heart contracted with pain. "As I have mentioned my mother has recently passed away. She was such a young and wonderful one too. I miss her. She was everything to me. There is no one else. I am fortunate that Digna has been like an aunt to me all of my life and has taken me in. I am very grateful." He swept his eyes across the canvas of her face and tried to picture Vermeer working on it. "Do you think you look like her?" As the words escaped, his tongue went to lead. It was obvious she had so much more of him, the fuller lips, arching brows, eyes almost the same color. She was the girl he would have been had he, luckily, not been born male. She was quick to answer. "No sir, I think we look not much alike, but I am tall like her. Many thought us perhaps sisters." Her turban was in perfect place. The white collar did not have a speck. Holland was a clean place and she was its poster child.

Gertrude tried to read their lips from behind the bar as she pretended to wash mugs. She surmised they were talking of Fleur's mother which seemed harmless enough. But she must have something to report to Maria. She needed to bide her time.

Later that evening Vermeer and Pieter sat in the darkest corner of the Mechelen, but Gertrude had her spying eye upon them. She dropped a tray near their table and feigned dismay. As she took her time to clean up she clearly heard Pieter ask Vermeer about his daughter's painting. Maria had not mentioned that he was painting their daughter Magdalena. She was not surprised, with so many portraits about the house, why not one of their own. Actually it was a nice idea. Perhaps Pieter is trying to surprise his wife and she is way off the mark barking up the wrong tree. How embarrassed and elated she will be if this is the situation. Perhaps she will be so gleeful she will want me to return. This would be regretful because Gertrude was actually enjoying her new employer and surroundings. She was thinking it may be the career she was destined for and could excel at. If only someone would at least do her silhouette. Perhaps Maria will give her a few guilders when this scenario comes to a close and the information she provides is desirable. Then she could hire a young artist. Everyone in her country loved art, it seemed, and so did she. Even though she heard the preachers call it the devil's work she thought it more godly. The two men had their heads very close now and it was getting difficult to discern what they were saying. Quietly she slipped into the kitchen to strip off a piece of the piggy roasting in the oven. Soon the Inn's patrons would devour it and she would have to suck on the bones.

CHAPTER 24

The poor girl was trembling. She could not speak. Her mouth opened, but nothing came out. Maria was at the edge of her seat. "Speak girl if you know what is in your best interest. If the cat has got your tongue the police will soon have you in custody." Gertrude was the most frightened she ever was in her simple life. Her palms were sweating and she could smell her bodily odor. "Ma'm I can only say they talk a good deal about the mother." Maria shot out of her seat like a toad. "What, Vermeer's mother? What in God's name?" Gertrude had to force herself to go on, so much was at stake. No Ma'm not his mother. Maria was more confused than ever. "Well who's? Pieter's mother has been dead for years." Gertrude blurted it out and was glad to be rid of the information. "Fleur's mother!" Maria was tossing her hands around in the air. Her jewels sparkled and lit up the room like expensive candles making the scene more dramatic. "But her mother is dead also." Gertrude was frustrated, but she groped for words and found them. "Not long, Ma'm." Maria put her face so close to Gertrude she could smell her moldy breath. "Did they say her name?" Gertrude nodded affirmatively, but forgot to speak. "Well spill it out girl." "Tessa, her name was Tessa. They talk much of a painting also. Vermeer will paint someone's daughter. It is very mixed up. I cannot get close. I did hear them say this will get the artist out of your debt and other bits and pieces about the painting and the mother." Maria felt weak. Her knees went to water. She sat down with a plop and yelled for the parlor maid to throw more wood on the fire. The large stone fireplace seemed as angry as she. It was red hot now. The warm air tried to reach them, but Maria's terror squelched all hope and the cold kept everyone at attention. She was suddenly very calm. Her voice went from a high pitch to almost a whisper. "This Fleur, she works at the Inn, the girl that Digna took in, the poor pitiful little orphan that no one else wanted." When she said this, her face wrinkled up like an old prune and her voice sounded snide as jealousy echoed behind every word. Once again she flew out of her seat. "You get to the bottom of this and I will see you next week or sooner if you have what I am after." With that she dismissed her and went back to her embroidery with a vengeance, without missing a stitch.

CHAPTER 25

This is when the Mechelen was most welcoming. The cauldron and fire burned in unison, hissing and popping, while sending aromatic smells of wild boar or hare through everyone's senses. The floors were scrubbed clean every day and night. The kitchen sparkled and Cook grumbled, no matter what. She sensed a change like a cat that smells a litter of rats five miles away. Her eyes are sharp too and she sees things. Her ears would challenge a fifteen-year-olds. They are her best friend and worst enemy, but her mouth is like a trap that opens only for the greater delicacy of wild fare. Instantly biting down before all this information she has inhaled will pour out like pins, needles and worst of all, snakes.

Gertrude entered Cook's domain like the sly, little ferret she was. "What's been keeping you, girl?" There are the potatoes and they are screaming, 'Peel me, peel me.' I got a headache listening." Gertrude looked clumsy and could not look her in the eyes. "I was just bringing Mr. Van Ruijven some dark ale to wash down your hot crusty bread, Ma'm." Cook looked at her like she had two heads. "What's all this talk and hanging around Mr. Van Ruijven and your mistress's son? I know you lived there, but have some pride, girl. They threw you out. You're quiet, but curious. These traits don't get you promoted at this establishment. Keep your hole shut like you do and keep your behind a plate's throw away from everyone. When you got that, you got something called a job. Fascination with older men only gets a girl in disgrace, or worse." When she turned back to her boiling pot Gertrude stuck out her tongue.

CHAPTER 26

Fleur was so surprised to have different feelings for the two new men in her life. When she was with the painter her breasts would tingle and it seemed her womanly parts became moist and tender. He was there, dark and light, no grey areas. Her stomach churned and was starving, but she could not eat more than a few bites. Exhausted and achy her bed was not a place to sleep, but to fantasize about the things he may do to her and how she might please him. Things no one really ever talked about. Her mother had hinted at intimacy between men and women in love, but she died too soon and the tale was never told in detail. At work, mugs turned into his face. When the door opened it was always him. His voice stood out in the loudest room although he was quiet. She wanted to be with him always.

But Pieter was different. She felt contentment around him. It was a very safe place to be. He would protect her, from what, she was not certain. Trust was complete. In her hour of need she could run to him without hesitation. She knew she could never count on Vermeer. Pieter was more than a friend, but it was definitely not romantic. She was stumped, but she liked the riddle of the two men. It helped keep her mind off her mother. Tessa would approve of both of them. They had the same ideals and tastes of her and her young mother. A look, a nod, a small gesture, words were an afterthought. They communicated with a special language all their own, they were that close. Suddenly she realized her first shift at the Mechelen was coming to an end and the second was devoted to Vermeer. She hurried to the storage room where he had already been working for hours on the curve of her lips.

CHAPTER 27

Delft was a small town with a lot of activity and business dealings that haggled on late into the night. The canals were the arteries of the town. All goods and exports were carried along here. They were flanked by the homes of merchants, traders, churches and institutions. The Mechelen stood on Marktveld, in a busy section of Delft. Many tradesmen, wealthy citizens and artists visited there regularly. Members of the Guild of St. Luke met to converse and pit one ale against the other. There seemed to be as much ale available as water in the canals. Delft literally means canals and these were reconnected with little islands and wooden stone bridges. Shade trees lined the canals, adorning clean and beautiful houses. Art would naturally flourish here for it brought to mind all things creative and aesthetic. The Renaissance was in full bloom and it was the Dutch Golden Age where a plethora of Dutch masters sought the blue ribbon of history in its most sought after category.

Vermeer was thinking about all of these things that kept him here. It was not the premier art center. The Hague, for example, outpaced Delft with its output of great paintings. Indeed many of his friends moved away for they felt cramped here and could not develop their craft. But he loved this city where his mother and friends supported him.

He was in the marketplace and everything was

so alive. All traces of the Thunderclap were gone and Delft was prospering. Porcelain tiles, tapestries and breweries were excelling. Tradesmen like the baker Van Buylen, headmaster of the Bakers Guild could afford to buy expensive paintings. In fact, the baker had purchased three of his, one where his wife was modeling in blue. It amazed him how the baker had risen like his dough. He had a house on the south side of Choostraat and one on Oudedelft and was in the process of purchasing two more. How could a baker stand above an artist? Perhaps he was a penny pincher and had a head for guilders. Johannes knew he could never concern himself exclusively with financial matters. It would ruin his artistic side. What a quagmire he was in. He almost wanted to run to the baker and trade more paintings for a ten year supply of white bread. He could feed his family and paint endlessly with no worries. But worry he did as he walked along the canal, anxious for the trees to reassert their authority and spread their braches wide, full of leaves and nests again. He could rest in a shady spot and forget he would always be struggling, unable to get ahead of his art. Then he thought of Fleur and his obsession with poverty turned to one of newfound love blotting out all other concerns. She had become his winter escape. He continued walking like a blind man with no care of obstacles in his way. He did not hear the butcher say good day or smell the blood hanging on his cuts of meat. He was imagining Fleur as his wife and was awakened with shame.

Then he realized that by painting her he would

possess her in another way. In a way no other man could.

CHAPTER 28

When Vermeer thought of women, it was never without pondering the importance and intricacies of their task. He painted because he literally wanted to capture the moment. The camera obscura helped him enhance his own ability to do so. It was the personal computer of his time catapulting his technique centuries ahead. Other artists that preceded him such as Da Vinci had tampered with the significance of boxes and lenses, understanding the scientific and intrinsically artistic benefit they would employ. He strove to show the world in its precise order. Loving detail, he could labor over the smallest section for weeks. Sometimes he forgot the bigger picture and became entombed in his passion. It was like driving tiny nails into his brain without a break, but still it brought him great pleasure. At three a.m. he would awaken and be anxious to start all over again.

In his self-portrait surrounded by friends, smiling and wearing his favorite cap as a disguise to tone down his identity, he thinks he has shown himself too handsome. He thinks he is not so. That was his interpretation. Each model must be enhanced to a certain degree. Art must have the advantage. People love beauty not truth.

He was thinking about these things in his most comfortable chair. He thought he might doze. There had been little time or desire for much needed sleep. He had just stoked the fire before settling in. Thinking of nothing, he just relaxed in the quiet and forgot about the complexities of his world. With the debt taken care of, he could afford to take some time to heal the soul that had been dragging the chains of financial hardship thru the market and to the Inn.

Suddenly when he could hear the distant river run and feel the arms of coziness engulf him Catarina came bursting in the room literally dropping their son in his lap. She was quite animated and her cheeks were rosy indicating she was worked up over some matter or the other. "Father, your son needs fatherly hugs and kisses. He wants you to put some paint on his fingers and go about on the walls to create baby's first mural." His wife was a fascinating woman. Her strength was a godsend for surely he had none. He looked at her with great reproach. "He may paint away a loaf of bread or slice of oxen in less than ten minutes time." Catarina's reply came without hesitation or care. "Well let us hope he finds an interest that pays a little higher wages than the trade you dabble in." She got up and left as quickly as she came leaving the boy behind. Just as the door shut, Vermeer could feel his son get very wet and warm in his seat. He could only laugh and say to himself, "remember this is how you started."

CHAPTER 29

The days moved ahead like light years. Vermeer painted incessantly. They laughed and talked and often just reveled in the silence of each other. But today enjoying their light conversation led them astray. Fleur was itchy and did not feel the role of model. "Will you ever be able to forget me? I will be burned into your memory with that next stroke." Dark eyes met hers and the unspoken truth roared like a white squall in the Atlantic. "I wish you could always be here when I come to paint and drink for I can do both for a long time." The quiet of the day was in great contrast to his thoughts; he could prolong this mission no longer. Pieter had been pleased; too pleased with the painting so far, he was putting great pressure on him for he wanted the painting to come to fruition. Fleur was unsettled. She could no longer contain herself, knowing how she felt. She wanted to run to him and lie with him upon the humble cot, bringing each other to a higher place. Vermeer's face looked solemn and whimsical at the same time. She braced herself for she knew he was about to say something they may both regret. "Fleur, you know I love you, but I can never have you." Fleur was not even stunned. The words she was about to speak did not tumble over each other as they should have. "You know that I love you, also, and will always be yours."

She stood and he came to her. He took off her turban and the braid she tucked inside fell down over her shoulders. Her brown hair was dark and would not have done so well in the painting. But in real life, it adorned her face like a beautiful prayer veil. They lay together on the cot. They did not even look at the painting. He kissed her, touching her face with the fingers that knew her so well. "Fleur, this can go no further." Her response was quick and sharp. "Then this is enough."

She took off her dress and lay in her simple undergarments, so they could be as close as possible, without committing adultery. He had never explored the body of a virgin, because his wife had been married before. She would have let him explore her further, but his conscience stopped him. She was sweet and warm, giving in a way that his wife never could. Yet if he was to lose her, which he must, he never would regret this moment.

"I do not believe in hell, Fleur, but now I am sure there is a heaven. This is it with you. If only it could go on forever." She could count thirteen reasons why it could not, his wife, eleven children, and of course, his mother in law.

CHAPTER 30

Windy and bright, full of blue sky, all this gave Pieter a reason to love Delft all the more. The market was a crowded hurry. The baker was arguing with a very fat woman in a dress that squeezed her like a sausage casing. She claimed he was selling her stale wares. It was like a sea of hats bobbing up and down in an ocean of people. He would have sent a servant, but these shoe buckles were pure gold and he wanted them delivered safe and sound to the cobbler. His coachman dropped the shoes off which were brought from the docks and had been imported from Spain. They were the rage and the buckles would add the flair he was famous for.

His love of all things beautiful had always been his downfall and pleasure, the double edge sword. Nothing else came his way, except for his wife. He could surround himself with the finest material things and did so with grace and insight. Art was the greatest of these loves, but it was a costly hobby. No, it was more like a passion. He was certain art was the medium that would move this millennium forward. It would lead humanity to exercise its mind and grow from appreciating to communicating on a higher level, perhaps accompanied by sound and movement. Words had not yet been penned that could express this new concept that went round in his mind like a mathematical equation he could almost solve. It would be an integral part of this fast growing world that this age of exploration was ushering in. Art was the predecessor that would command a future, shocking and foreign to inhabitants of planet earth today.

Occasionally he would see a familiar face that brought him out of his thoughts. A nod, a quick tip of the hat, he smiled and dazzled all the women to this day. "Look there," exclaimed a petite young maiden carrying a basket full of geese and pudding. "Pieter Van Ruijven is still so handsome. He ages like a wine and cheese upon the finest porcelain. The combination is perfect." He pretended not to hear, but it made his heart glad that he was not looking like he should be out to pasture.

A cart hurried by, its horse's hooves kicking up dirt. Quickly he slipped out of the way. Just as it passed he had a vision. Fleur stood across the street. She was accompanied by the maid Maria had dismissed. They were haggling over some cloth, possibly for use at the Mechelen. Her profile was perfectly carved as if by Michelangelo. She seemed immersed in the moment so he slipped past the girls and continued towards the cobbler. When he looked back she had turned away, but he would know her from any angle. She was his child.

Later today, Johannes was showing him the progress. He loved Thursday. It was now his favorite. He did not want to push Vermeer, but he knew he could. Pieter wanted to move the mountains, tear up trees and swallow waterfalls to make this happen. Perhaps he could draw strength from the painting, eventually telling Fleur the true story. It would be like a blood transfusion if such a thing could be done, and would be someday, he was certain. He would rise from his condition and claim what was his. He would change his will and build her a sturdy cottage surrounded by cutting gardens. He would visit her every week with candies and small conversation all construed to be in her company.

The cobbler's bell rang too loudly in his ears ruining his daydreams. The little man hurried from behind the green patched up curtain. He was bald and craggy like the moon. Pieter almost forgot why he was there until he remembered the package in his back pocket. The shoemaker shuffled back and forth nervously as Pieter handed him the buckles and hurried away. Gustaf wondered what was wrong. He did not make small talk, which was his custom or ask for an estimate. Well, that is what it was like to be a rich man in Delft. Something he would never know.

CHAPTER 31

Vermeer did not sleep that last night, or warm the fires in the storage room, with new logs. He sat suspended just evaluating the painting and knowing the end had come. He tried to do an honest appraisal, but he was far too emotional. He did not care what all the critics in Holland would think. Those Dutch masters have never achieved such excellence in all their tedious attempts. Without Fleur as a subject, how could they? He explored her every detail, commanding them to memory; the arch of her light brow, the way she teased him with a look that would torment him for the rest of his life. He felt a moment of betrayal to his wife, but had no care. The earring became the mirror he would hide in. His reflection would never be revealed, but he would travel with her till destiny would one day reunite them.

Her face was his. He had caressed it and slid his finger along the gentle curve of her nose, the plumpness of her lips. He wanted to nibble on her chin, like an apple, and keep the taste in his mouth; going without dinner so he would not lose her scent. Out of the darkness came the light. "I found my way now, but yet I will lose her." She had led him into the golden age. "The climax is sweet as my hand against her plentiful breasts. Will the world look upon her as I do? Will my secret be revealed in her eyes? Can I share such beauty? I want to be a miser and keep her for myself. I cannot bear that after today she will belong to someone else." The night grew old and tired of Vermeer. It coaxed him to say goodbye before the sun appeared, torching all of his hopes and desires. He picked up the cover and placed it lightly over the painting. Regretfully he walked out of her life and hurried home where Catarina, the mother of his children, slept soundly in their bed.

CHAPTER 32

It was very early in the morning. Vermeer was up and ready to tell his mother the entire truth. Gertrude was also awake and preparing pots and utensils for Cook. Digna was surprised to see her son at the door. The dawn was painting him, and he glowed and looked almost young again. But when she saw the expression on his face she could see he was in a serious mood. As she thought these words, he approached her. "Mother, are we alone? We need to speak." The cold air had followed him and when the door slammed Gertrude was alerted. She peeped out into a scene that Vermeer may have titled "Mother and Artist's Dawn." She smelled the urgency. "Mother I know you realize I am working for Pieter Van Ruijven in the storage area. I have let on that he needs a typical Dutch girl for the guild." Gertrude's ears seemed to grow out of her head like ant antennas. She was as still as the mouse hiding from the cat. Vermeer hesitated for the moment. The Inn was eerily still, sleeping, finally rested from last night's festivities that went on into the wee hours. "As I said he has agreed to cancel out the debt. Pieter has looked upon the final touches with much approval and I am certain that this has legally released me from further encumbrance. He is a man of his word." Digna made a soft sigh of relief. "This is wonderful, but how have we come upon such good fortune?" The son studied his mother's once beautiful face with its high cheekbones and God-given fine bone structure. Yet the years had gathered up the sorrows and hard work painted lines and a tired look about her mouth and eyes. His circumstances had not enhanced her, but she was always there for him like his favorite brush whose bristles wear down long before the rest. He started to speak, but it was difficult to expel the words. "This is a great secret, and one you must take to your grave." He hung up his hat and cloak and motioned for her to sit at her famous oak carved bar, the longest in Delft. It boasted scenes of Dutch men of the day sitting around big barrels talking, gesticulating and of course drinking beer. This was a lucky move for Gertrude with the kitchen being very near to them, and they suspected nothing. He looked into his mother's eyes where they lingered for what felt like an eternity to Gertrude. "Fleur is the natural daughter of Pieter Van Ruijven. He was never informed of her birth. Tessa, your friend, was the love of his life, but you know how it is. Yes, he regrets his choice, but he is weak, the only flaw in his perfectly cut diamond. At the time he could not find a way to stand against his father's rule. Unlike Pieter, his father was like the Rock of Gibraltar, sturdy and harsh, nothing passed by his watchtower or powerful domain. Deep down inside I believe Pieter is still convinced he has not lived up to his father's expectations." Digna was reeling and could not at first reply. Her son continued, now seeming in a hurry to blurt out the rest of the tale. "He does not know if or when he will tell her, but he is jubilant I tell you, and his life has come full circle. Ironically, the painting means everything to him and me." Digna was smiling now, looking ten years younger. All of her teeth were intact and they seemed happy also. "And me as well, Son. This represents a fresh start. You can concentrate on your other works with this weight lifted. You will one day be acclaimed the greatest artist in all of Europe, one of the greatest who ever lived. You must know I have felt this since you were a young boy drawing in your school books. Even when the schoolmaster paddled you, the art kept showing up." They both shared a good laugh before she continued, "I am in deep shock, but I will pull myself together. I shall never repeat this to a living soul, I assure you. My wise lips know when to remain silent. Your father Reyiner taught me much of discretion." They both relaxed for a moment sitting in silence while a bird sang a sweet melody calling its friends to join his flight into spring. Digna spoke with the wisdom that her son expected, "now that this has been revealed to me I can see the resemblance. Honestly, Tessa did hint to me of Fleur's paternity, but we had an unspoken agreement and though I suspected I never prodded." Johannes was praying she could not read his feelings about Fleur. She was a very perceptive woman, but luckily her busy life dulled her once highly active sixth sense. Yes, he thought this will free Pieter, but it is enslaving me for I cannot escape the thought or want of her.

Gertrude had heard enough, next she would move forward with her afternoon plan. She had been shocked and felt like a statue that lightening had struck. It was time to get moving with the ammunition needed to rid herself of this horrible mission. Unfortunately, she had grown to admire Fleur and was abhorred to follow through on this dastardly deed. But her choices had dwindled down. Listen and tell. Soon Maria would be a bad dream from the past, but life would go on. Suddenly she felt her collar being tugged at from behind. As she turned around there was Cook holding the rolling pin. "The door isn't going to do the work for you my dearie. Get to your station. You darn well know I have to leave early today and there is much to do. Now, or this rolling pin will be tattooed onto your behind. Flying rolling pins and angry Cook are not something that will make your pretty little heart glad." The sparkling kitchen was lit up by the rising sun. It warmed up the room like butter spread on morning toast. For the first time in months Gertrude discovered a newfound energy like a sailor who had just sighted land after months at sea.

As she hid behind the old thick curtains in the storage area she could not believe that fate had brought her to a solution in one day after a winter of anticipation. She had seen Pieter and Vermeer come and go. They seemed to have a set schedule that revolved around guild meetings. Every Thursday, exactly at noon, they entered this room. Digna had gone to the market with Cook to pick up their secret ingredients for tonight's meals. It was not often that she was left alone and was determined to take the opportunity. She had snuck in through the cracked window that led from the kitchen. No one had time to repair it and this worked in her favor. She longed to see the painting for herself. Her mind was racing faster than a greyhound in a dead heat. The room was dark so she struck a candle to inspect. There, illuminated against the flame was the unmistakable gaze of Fleur.

The portrait was almost complete and she finally had all of the information and proof. Soon she would scurry to Maria and divulge the damning tale.

The two men had just left and she had heard it all loud and clear. Pieter was almost in tears begging Vermeer to hurry so he could be close to his beautiful daughter. He wanted her near him even if it was just in effigy. Johannes assured Pieter the work was progressing nicely. He felt quite vigorous and was painting seven days a week managing to work on Sundays after mass. Fleur was a hard working girl much like her father and all would be well. He went on to comment on how as he painted her, he realized how much more she looked like him than Tessa. Pieter went on to explain that he had no idea Tessa had conceived Fleur and was ecstatic to have found her. He had deeply loved Tessa and now he would have an earthly connection with her. Had he known about the child, he may have gone down a completely different path in life, one filled with love, happiness and true honor. Tessa's death was like a dagger left in his heart, but Fleur had removed it and given him back a reason to live.

CHAPTER 33

Mrs. Van Ruijven took the information better than Gertrude had expected. The puzzle now fit together a little too neatly. Fleur was Pieter's daughter. That was the information that would finally release her from the witch's grasp. Maria said little and told her to return in a week's time. She should be finished with her by then. When she came back the following week at the designated time, she could not imagine what more Maria could want. This was playing over and over in her mind as she waited in the foyer. Looking around she found herself immersed in a world she could only visit. It was a tease to have lived in such surroundings and never partake. When she was a servant, she lived inside a bubble, inside a house that did not wish you to speak; the doorknob having a higher position than she. At least at the tavern she felt alive and it was a believable existence. She could rise to the position of inn keeping. That would be respectable and she could live modestly. There was nothing modest about this place. Every detail of the Van Ruijven house screamed rich. There were paintings crowding the walls in perfect splendor. Delft porcelain was placed about the rooms in harmony. Wood railings and walls were polished to the highest shine. Servants were busy pursuing their master's wishes morning, noon and night. She could hear a harpsichord playing in a distant room. Magdalena, the daughter, played beautifully considering she seemed not to have a soul. When Gertrude worked at the house, the homely Magdalena loved to pull off her wings and she did so with ease. The tea was never hot enough; the biscuits were dry. Her dress was too wrinkled. Gertrude swore she tore off buttons from her dresses so that Gertrude would have to sew them back on again and again. She was endlessly scrubbing spots out of the sloppy girl's extravagant gowns. There was no end to her tortures. This torture was almost better. Just as she was drifting away with her thoughts, she was summoned into Maria's personal chambers. Everyone left the room immediately.

Maria looked frightening. She had dark circles under her eyes. They were puffy and leathery. She lost weight which seemed impossible considering she always kept herself bird-thin. It looked as if she had not eaten meat nor slept in a year. "Gertrude, I will not mince words. You will take Fleur to the canal and you will drown her or so help me God you will rot in hell, right here in Delft."

Gertrude felt as if the floors had opened up and would swallow her right then and there. She could hear teeth gnashing and devils laughing. Suddenly she felt like fainting, but thought she might ask for a glass of water instead. Instantly, Maria rang the maid's bell, and Gertrude managed to remain standing. Nothing was up for discussion.

CHAPTER 34

The canal had just broken up and melted. The rowboat glided across the water. Gertrude was strong. Her breasts heaved in unison with her femininely muscular arms and hands that gripped the oars like an expert rower. Fleur looked peaceful. Gertrude could see the calmness beneath her confidant poise. It was all too romantic and Mrs. Van Ruijven wanted her dead. She had all the power because she had all the money.

Fleur came out of her daydream. "Gertrude, you are quite athletic. You would never know it by the way you handle a tray of ale." She laughed and it was contagious. Gertrude could not help agreeing. But she soon remembered the task at hand, and her heart was once again aching. The day was quiet. Spring was in its infancy. You could almost hear the daffodil bulbs tapping the ground demanding entrance into its familiar world. Gertrude had to ask her if she knew. It was only fair she knew before she...

"Fleur, why do you think Pieter Van Ruijven takes such an interest in a tavern maid?" Fleur's eyes opened like a jaguar, suddenly sighting its prey in the tall grass. "Why do you think such a thing? He is a customer, and we need to make his time at the Mechelen most pleasant." Suddenly Gertrude's face darkened and changed as if she put on a dark mask for a ball. "You know he is your natural father. It is true." Fleur could not digest the words. Her head jerked back from the crack of the whip of truth. She felt like screaming, crying, laughing, all at once. "How? Why?" It didn't matter. There was no more denying that something that had tugged at her like a song on Valentine's Day. He was hers and that was enough. Valentine's Day may only last a moment, but she would always keep the song close to her heart, where nobody could steal it away from her. Gertrude, meanwhile, was thinking too hard. The words were spinning around like a windmill, going as fast as possible without jettisoning out into a field killing the farmland.

Maria had this terrible thing over her head. Surely she would go to jail. No one would come to help her. She would die there or get the pox for sure and later die a more horrible death. "And now that you know this, you must know the worst. His wife wants me to kill you here and now. Throw you into the canal and make it look like you drowned accidentally or perhaps committed suicide. She has set me up, laying the pieces on the chess board so she is in a perfect position. She will win. You and I are just pawns in her wicked game. No bishop will save us."

Fleur could not listen. She thought Gertrude her friend. "You are not nosey for nothing, then Gertrude" said Fleur. "You have stalked me like a wild animal of the Inn. She is this mean to make others turn upon me for a transgression of so long ago." Gertrude's reply came fast and hard. "She will prevail and there is no time to chatter about it. You must leave Delft now! But first I must have your earrings as proof that you are dead."

This was the most painful task that Fleur had ever performed. The earrings seem to be a part of her now. They swung when she rushed happily around the Inn. They nestled on her face as she slept. They were a part of her mother and father, all she had of them. But her life depended on her not having them, and Gertrude's life as well. Then she remembered that she had worn them for Johannes. He had painted them into the portrait. They would never disappear. One would never fall off and leave the other behind in sadness as her father had left Tessa. This was great consolation and she handed them to Gertrude with no regrets. Gertrude looked at Fleur and found it hard not to cry. She liked sleeping near her in her trundle bed, but that would be no more. Her nights would again be lonely, and when Maria was in her nightmares there would be no solace from Fleur. She would be gone, but she felt better when she realized gone was not dead.

CHAPTER 35

Pieter could not stop looking at the painting. It was perfect. She looked right at him. This was all he wanted. He had found her and that was enough for now. He had to digest all of his feelings. Fleur had to be treated with special gloves. It might be too painful for her to have this revealed at such a time. Tessa had not been dead a year. Not now. He will adore her from afar and find a way to help make her life more comfortable. Johannes will help him; he must and do so with great secrecy and tact. His mother will give her a raise and new comfortable tavern shoes. Every Sunday and Monday she will have off to explore her other interests and find out who she really is. Of course, this he could fund. It would be of little consequence to his purse. His coffers are full of generations of brewery money. Finances are in order and grow without much effort. The machine keeps moving as his fortune rises like the tide of Biscayne Bay. Yet love runs through his fingers like the sand the tide kissed and then abandons before the sunrise. Could love ever reign in his lifetime? He is tired of the money. It is boring, yet no one likes a softly woven, fur lined cape more than he does. Alas, the puzzle gets more difficult to solve. The portrait comes back into focus and his countenance changes to that of absolute contentment and resolve. Life can only be good with Fleur in it.

As Pieter was enjoying his painting, elation was taking over. His hearth gave him great solace and he finally felt comfortable in his own home. But downstairs flames danced before Maria tauntingly, calling her names, mocking her very existence. Surrounding her at the height of elegance and charm were various oak carved furnishings. The detail and workmanship were beyond compare. Silk flowers sat upon her oak coffer. She should have been the most comfortable woman in Delft, but she might as well have been wearing a penance sack of horsehair. She was holding her favorite Delft charger. It was a round plate with crest markings. Upon it was painted a landscape scene depicting a tall house and chimney among trees. The oversized whimsical bird perched on a limb. If she was that bird she would fly away to find a new life with a mate that loved her. That would be the only requirement. She had enough money. So why did she not marry a man who just wished to spend his life in enjoyment with her? If only she could leave this monstrous house behind with all of its trappings. She had trapped Pieter and now she was miserable. It had become a house of horrors. Loveless and empty, misery looked in every corner for her. Her spouse may as well have been the butler for all of his affection toward her.

Yet, there was some consolation. Pieter and she shared a mutual love of art. Their Renaissance furniture reflected this as well as all of the wall hangings. There were ornate carvings on chairs, table legs and cabinets. They were all adorned with figures. Some pieces were imported from Italy at great cost. She loved the rectangular table with scrolling on the legs. Something new called upholstery was her favorite. She would sink into her favorite chair. Leather appeared on Pieter's' seat which was as of late empty. She found this material to be masculine and made its empty presence all the more intolerable. Gertrude's news was growing in her brain like a tumor. The pain was unbearable and he did not even notice her behavior. No, the servants were more attentive than he ever was. It was not that he was cruel. He was polite and played the role of husband superficially and socially. They had a daughter, but had not been intimate since her birth fourteen years ago.

She would have her revenge. Pieter would be sorry he had ever laid eyes on the tavern slut or entered the cursed inn called the Mechelen. The story would not have a fairy tale ending, of this she was certain.

CHAPTER 36

The last Vermeer saw was the wave of her hand as the cart pulled away, slowly like it was full of lead. His heart weighed down and he knew it was now over. She had been so frightened at his door, pretending to have a message to deliver from his mother. What a clever girl. This would get her through. He told her not to go back to the Mechelen. She would go to The Hague to live with his blind master. He needed a woman to care for him and it would be good that he could not identify her easily. The Guild was sending supplies as they did regularly; oil and brushes, frames and canvases that needed repair. She would ride with them to their destination and never return. Maria was vindictive and more than clever, cunning. If she meant to kill Fleur, she would at every turn.

Dusk waited a little tonight. The sun was golden like his angel. It wanted to linger over the canals, warming them up after the cruel winter. All around town the flowers were trying to take over. The march was full force and defeat wonderful. Vermeer would be their prisoner for now, but he would always steal their colors, and they could not stop him. But Fleur was no longer among them. He would never bring her back. But he was comforted by the fact that wherever she went his light would followl persevering the texture and depth of their forbidden love.

CHAPTER 37

The entrance to the Delft mansion was icy cold. Pieter looked around as he entered. He remembered his pledge to start warming up his foyer with more tapestries. They grace every other room it seemed, but the most important. Tapestries could be welcoming and warm; his guests would find refuge and fine dining here at his home. Perhaps he would have his crest embossed on the one that would hang above the door for the sake of his father and ancestors that haunted his breweries. Strange, Maria had a penchant for meeting him at the door. Odd, but this thought passed like a bee, busy to get back to the hive. Well the queen bee would soon seek him out. That was certain. Her painfully dull eyes and snobbish demeanor would be around each corner. He saw no way out, yet. At least now when he returned to his private quarters he could examine Fleur. Vermeer had created a masterpiece as much as he and Tessa had. The girl was the painting and the painting was the girl. Last night after Vermeer delivered the final work, he sat in utter delight. Studying his child, he tried to envision her in a field of tulips as a three-year-old. She would pick all of the pink ones and bring him one. He saw himself tossing her in the air and laughed like a rainbow.

She was every color to him. Fleur was more important than his life's work at the brewery and far more sacred than his family. Only Tessa remained above her, the light that united them into the trinity of true family. He did not want to look upon Fleur until after dinner. He could not bear seeing her and his wife in tandem tonight. Their own daughter Magdalena would be there complaining of some unimportant matter, such as a lack of gold lace in her wardrobe, while all of her friends had plenty. He was quite hungry, surprisingly. It felt good to come to an amenable end to the Vermeer debt, at least Vermeer's debt to him. And at the end he had gotten the bargain. At last he had found Fleur, Fleur for an eternity.

The lights were dim tonight in the grand dining room. Magdalena looked a bit more chipper than expected. He kissed her on the cheek and greeted Maria casually sitting at his accustomed kingly spot. The soup was boiling hot and this was a surprise. The kitchen had been built at a distance since most fires started there, potentially burning down the entire house. The servants had to dash across the lawn even on the coldest days unable to serve the food fast enough to their famished masters. Maria was being very odd tonight and kept tapping her spoon annoyingly on her plate. She called to the servant, suddenly asking him to light the three candles in front of her.

He was glad for more light, wanting to see what smelled so delicious. Before he could get his first bite, Maria called his name. It sounded like it was coming from another dimension, but she was right there in front of him. Looking up he felt a shock that riveted across the continent. He dropped his spoon in an instant. His face fell like a raven shot dead out of its happy perch. There,

94

upon her ears, were Fleur's earrings, dangling like two people hung from the scaffold of love, Pieter and Tessa.

Chapter 38

The police investigator was measuring up the old lady from the Mechelen kitchen. She had quite a story or perhaps a tale. It was true he had not seen the willowy tavern maid about. Such lovelies are swept away daily by anxious young men searching for pleasant wives. It had crossed his mind this would not take long when he watched her perform her duties with such grace and dignity. He often stopped in for quick ale when he was off duty. Crime was something that never failed to give him thirst. The harder he labored the more he drank at night. The amount of drink was in direct proportion to his caseload. Only his meager wages remained constant and steadily reminded him of his duty. He needed to protect the Dutch citizens from themselves. Now, that there was no war, society had too much time on its hands. Hence, he rose to the present position, fighting crime like it was the aftermath fire of the Delft Thunderclap.

Cook was struggling to get her shawl around the expanse of her back like Magellan attempting to circumvent the globe. She was grunting and making last minute remarks in between. If she could be of any help, please come to the Inn. She smelled a rat. The trail could start there and lead them to where Fleur had gone before the scent was extinguished forever. No one knew how quickly the hand of time could ravage a crime scene more than him. Traces and bits and pieces would disappear like the victim, but he had a knack for reconstructing scenarios with minute clues and quickly spoken words. He could ferret out the truth from the most skilled, compulsive liars. They were no match for his natural ability to observe and surmise. He had created science gathering evidence like a robin collecting twigs and strings for her nest.

When the other officers looked upon him that day they could not see the calculations starting to formulate under his unruly head of hair. Although he was barely taller than his desk and his little blue eyes seemed ordinary, they knew better. He did not have a long nose for nothing and ears that matched. They protruded through his scanty long hair giving him a feral look. His files were as thick as several bales of hay all tied up in old cords and almost in alphabetical order. All marked solved, save the one he just opened and signed after Cook's departure. Curious, one of the junior officers walked behind his desk reading the title, "The Mysterious Case of the Missing Mechelen Maid." He was quite envious knowing it would take decades to catch up with this master of the criminal chase. More importantly he was determined to learn all he could before death or retirement would rob the department of the master's expertise.

Officer Vootenstrass was still mulling over details that night at dinner, which he had gleaned thus far from Cook's statement. It was not the least bit difficult for him to think and eat. His wife was married to him long enough and remained quiet. She never asked questions for she feared all things violent. A policeman should have been her last choice for a husband. Yet, he had provided her a good life even without the blessing of children. The Lord had given her a fine man instead.

Tomorrow he thought he would go to the Mechelen and for once refrain, for I shall be on duty. Digna, I will question first for she had sent Cook to deliver the message. Young maidens do not fall from the earth like apples from the trees. Not one body has washed up from the canals or been found in the woods or alleys. If she ran off with a fellow she would have needed her wardrobe. Prices are dear and young fools could afford little. She left even guilders behind. Cook said not one item was gone from her room. She disappeared with the clothes on her back and turban on her head.

He thanked his goodly wife for the comforting meal and settled into his home desk. It was scratched and worn as an old shoe. He could not always think at the precinct with all the revolving sounds of police and suspects loudly proclaiming their innocence. He opened the drawer and placed the book he retrieved next to the hot toddy, which his wife had just provided in her familiar discreet manner. The cover was very feminine made out of what looked like a material called caffa. It was very busy with flowers of many colors and types. Vines wrapped around the border adding to its beauty, which gave it a flavor of enchantment. This could very easily hold the key that will provide the answer to the girl's whereabouts. Cook was right about that. Without hesitation he opened up Fleur's diary and began to read…

Chapter 39

The Mechelen was not well lit and cold. It was early in the morning. Detective Vootenstrasse had made it a point to come to the inn when there were no patrons about making all kind of ruckus. He could think when he could hear. Although in reality his mind never stopped working. In his sleep the matters of crime ran relentlessly around and around. He tried to ignore it when he was off duty. But there was no rest for a man of his intelligence and caliber. His brain worked harder than his heart. He did not have time for romance and such nonsense. What he did have was a healthy wife to cook his victuals and warm him up on a frosty winter's night. They both had given up on intimate matters years ago in mutual agreement. Alandra, his wife, was relieved to be spared this task which he sensed she always feared. Occasionally, a young Dutch beauty popped up from the fertile land of Holland before his eyes and he was sad that he would never know her or see what pleasantries lay beneath her feminine apron. He marveled at the information he had gathered thus far. It added up, all the little pieces from corners and cracks. A splattering here and then there was the diary. He would hold that as tight as an ace. Every word would be dissected and run through the sorting process of his mind. It was as important to him as the Magna Carta had been to the people of eleventh century England. Every word was critical and could not be misconstrued. All evidence must be weighed and dissected like a naturalist struggling to understand the inner workings of a beetle.

Outside the air was still crisp but there was no stopping the force of nature that gave and took season after season. It was fickle, but at the same time constant. This did not make sense but it was a fact, like murders never make sense, but they kept on occurring, no matter what the season. There was never a good time or bad time to kill. Summer's excuse was the heat, winter the holidays, spring unrequited love. Lastly, there was autumn when everyone was depressed dreading the winter ahead. The business kept coming through the door at the precinct. There was no need for salesmen. Crime had a life all of its own and renewal was automatic. Business was always booming. If he had a guilder for every madman hung in Holland over the past five years he could retire and fulfill his passion for writing detective stories. But he would be too old by then. Perhaps someone would murder him if he did not hurry up and catch all of the bad citizens of Delft in his quick and efficient manner. However, for now, he was not convinced he had a killing on his hands. Yes, someone seemed to have wanted to kill Fleur or perhaps kidnap her. But kill----he was not convinced. No body, no bloody weapon. There was not even a crime scene. He started his brainstorming board back at the office. He drew the faces of all suspects. Immediately he added all other pertinent information in an orderly fashion. Coaching the young officers in the pursuit of the truth became contagious. They eagerly added their own ideas and information that they sensed would lead to solving the mystery. Although his caricatures were cartoonish there was uniqueness in his drawings. Eventually he would draw the truth and the criminals would be convicted, jailed or hung. Whatever someone else decided, that was not his job. He was on the hunt like the bobcat who will seek his prey late into the night. He could be as nocturnal as an owl. And he could be as early of a riser as a dairy maid, whatever it took to uncover the truth.

The door had barely squeaked when he entered the establishment. He did not make grand entrances. He wanted to look around unnoticed, blending into the woodwork he could investigate unnoticed. He could observe, synthesize, add, subtract and formulate. Then he would file the pertinent information into one the numerous folds of his brain for future analysis. The first thing to register in his beady blue eyes was all of the knick knacks and beer steins scattered around in happy disharmony. There were some that dated back hundreds of years and some were missing lids or broken pieces. This did not distract from the enjoyment they sought when filled up with fine beers and ales. It was a big place with thick beams and stucco walls that made a man feel like one when he entertained his friends here.

The famous bar, the longest in Delft, was built and carved by highly skilled craftsman. It was easy to drink your fill here and settle into a well-worn bench to raise a glass. Perhaps you just wanted to relax to shut out the outside world and the odious things in life that kept you coming back for a refill. Vootenstrasse tried to picture Fleur the last time he saw her. She was upstairs and since he was a police officer he had the rare privilege of being welcomed on both floors. She was carrying a tray full of stew and warm wine. She seemed happy and full of energy. Her pretty face was wearing a big smile and she glowed in the half lit room like chandeliers filled with candles lit for the holiday. There was no stopping her as she glided back and forth meeting the demands of all of the customers equally.

Then he remembered the dark man behind her; it was just a glimpse. It was odd the way he followed the girl. Officer Vootenstrasse felt unsettled but tonight he put that thought away for later consideration.

Chapter 40

Digna was a frail woman, but officer Vootenstrasse knew that belied a soul of steel. As she walked gingerly toward him, he observed her hands were tightly clutching a hanky. He felt a pang of pity, which was a foreign feeling. It worked against his ethics to allow these frivolous thoughts. But it was as fleeting as a fly that lands on your nose till you swipe it away. Digna's voice was sad but she tried her best to be cordial "Come upstairs detective. Gertrude will bring us some hot rolls and milk." The detective had seen the goats herded behind the Inn. The milk will be as fresh as the morning dew.

Gertrude never took her eyes off Detective Vootenstrasse. She was overjoyed that he seemed such a clumsy, silly little man. She had never seen a funnier fellow. Yet, her heart was pounding wildly under her ample bosom. Trying to pour dark ale, she missed completely as she glanced back and forth like a very hungry owl in search of a fat cat. She continued to watch as the pair went to the upper level, where they could occupy a private booth.

After refusing any spirits the detective quickly cut to the chase. "Digna," he said, his little teeth showing like little puppets under his mustache. "Truthfully, did you have anything to do with Fleur's disappearance? Duty does not know valor"

Digna inhaled and held her breathe for what seemed like an hour. Without hesitation she shook her head to affirm what he had already deducted. She had shown the girl kindness and he could extrapolate no motive from any of the evidence thus far. Digna's eyes teared up and she took another delicate hanky from the cuff of her dress to wipe them. Then she went on to assure him that she was as shocked and mystified as others of Fleur's disappearance. The greatest burden was the promise she had made her mother to care for the girl and keep her safe, a death bed promise. The door opened downstairs and Gertrude was surprised to see Vermeer's wife sweep past her and up the steps. She was in such a hurry her ringlets were bouncing keeping time with each and every step.

Digna was also surprised when Catarina approached the booth. "Oh, Detective Vootenstrasse, I would like to introduce you to my daughter-in-law Catarina." Catarina tilted her head and smiled, making her appear angelic in the morning light. "Oh yes, we have met before at the Guild of St. Luke's annual drive for the police." The detective quickly responded, "your husband has done much to help us catch the thieves who may in fact attempt to steal important works of art. I assure you madam they have on numerous occasions." Suddenly Catarina seemed perplexed and stopped. "Mother," for a moment she rummaged thru her bag, "I am perplexed." "How did you end up with my windmill as a decoration for the Mechelen?" The windmill sat precariously on a small shelf just out of the officer's reach. Digna shrugged and flung her hand about like she was swatting a gnat. "It is of little importance compared to the disappearance of Fleur. But if you must know, Maria Van Ruijven presented it to me when I accepted Gertrude as a tavern maid. She was so relieved to be rid of her as a household servant she gave it to me. It almost felt like bribery. However, it had little effect for I do not have use for such trinkets. It was just one more knickknack to dust. "You say it is yours?" Catarina looked perplexed. "Yes, I bartered with Maria in exchange for an important favor." Catarina became very quiet and cast her eyes onto old, but shiny black boots. Digna was surprised she had found time or money for polish. Digna quickly changed the subject knowing that Catarina was embarrassed by her husband's debt.

Chapter 41

That night Officer Vootenstrasse cut up his puzzle cards, as he called them. Luckily, his mother had been raised in a convent and was an excellent teacher. She was also very observant and had a great many powers. He believed she could hear a blade of grass grow, with her overgrown ears so much like his. He wrote down every detail two times, three times, if he felt it may be pivotal. The same word stumbled about in his mind. Windmill, windmill, windmill. Why? Maria Van Ruijven, Gertrude the maid, Catarina the wife, Cook, Digna, the two men in her life. What was the connection? How do they blend into the case? Who has the motive, opportunity, cold bloodedness or could Fleur have run off? Nonsense. He took his tea bag and squeezed. If only tea leaves could provide answers for him as they did for Caesar's soothsayers, nonsense. There is only logic, reason, natural occurrences, patterns, human behavior and most importantly, human error. He would find that loose thread and break it down until the truth was found no matter how deeply it was sewn in the fabric.

Chapter 42

The rage that Pieter felt could be sensed by every member of the staff. The downstairs servants quivered as they dusted every speck twice over. You could not find a fingerprint in the household. Maria was rarely seen for over a week. She languished in her bedroom and played solitaire incessantly. The only thing that passed her lips were crackers and hot milk. Occasionally, she would ask for a small piece of fine Danish cheese to be spread in a precise amount that did not exceed the size of a wisp of hair. She had won a great battle. But oh how the love for Pieter still ripped her into miniscule pieces. How she had not yet died of some disease related to her misery was beyond comprehension. Even the King Charles beagles looked up at her as if to say why do you not take us for a walk far away? We can sail back to London together and look for their mother. Oh how they adored her and she them. Their little warm bodies gave her hope because she could feel their happiness and it was a balm.

She still wore the earrings; never would they leave her person. She had earned them. Of course, she would have been happier to see the body as it dropped to the bottom of the canal. Gertrude was very smart for weighing the body down with a big meat pounder and various other heavy kitchen items. Without Gertrude her task would have been difficult. But Gertrude had done surprisingly well and exceeded all of Maria's expectations. She had forgotten about Tessa, the rumors, the sorrowful groom, a honeymoon of horrors. Pieter had not touched her for months after they were married. She had to catch him off guard the time she became pregnant with Magdalena. It was a quiet, snowy evening. He was in a rare mood. She read him Cicero and coaxed him into tasting several ports that she had special ordered from Portugal. The ruby red liquid acted upon him like a love potion. He followed her to her quarters and asked to play with the puppies. As they frolicked with them in the down bed that was fit for any princes she fell into his arms. For one moment she thought he may have relented and decided to give the marriage a try. Instead she woke up to an empty pillow and a man colder than the glaciers of Iceland.

When Magdalena was born Pieter dutifully gave all of his friends the finest cigars and brandy. He did not ever seem disappointed that it was not a boy. He was almost happy it was a girl. This way he would not be expected to dote on her, which he never did.

She was more worried now about Pieter's anger than ever getting caught. Her family was powerful and their tentacles reached to the heart of ever magistrate in Delft where they squeezed just hard enough for everyone to keep their place. One more tightening of the grip and men in high places would succumb to more pain than they cared to feel. Guilders solved all of her problems. She had a family that protected her like the castle guards protected the King of England. There was not a person in Delft who could touch her. But then again she had never met Detective Vootenstrasse who was at that very moment scribbling her name on his last puzzle card for the night. He placed it under his pillow and closed his eyes. As he started his slumber a thought took hold. It wormed its way into his logical brain where it felt right at home.

Chapter 43

Sweat and tears roused Pieter out of a deep sleep that enveloped him like a witch's cauldron. He could barely open his eyes. His stomach was still there; he could feel its emptiness. It did not matter for he would surely vomit if he ate. He wanted to die anyway. The dream kept coming back. Tessa was reaching out for him. Her blond hair was wrapped in a halo and her light skin glowed against the darkness of the Netherworld. She was calling out for Pieter to find Fleur, but her eyes and mouth were closed. Her arms extended reaching for him, pleading. When she opened her eyes they were empty, blue orbs of this world forgotten or left behind. With this he would wake and tremble under the weight of his own misery. Not a soul had seen Fleur. It was almost like a Shakespearean tragedy. The painting complete and the heroine disappears. He kept seeing Maria wearing the earrings. Haughty, laughing, she had killed Fleur. He was certain. Maria will not divulge a syllable. How can he go to the police? He will be ruined. They will think him mad. How can he prove anything with the nothingness that is left behind? He will beat the truth out of Maria. He will lock her in a closet until she breaks. His hatred for her is like an active volcano ready to erupt and spew poisonous gas and molten lava upon anything in his path. He seethes and tosses and turns. Pieter's eyes burn like a pirate's lantern calling in ships to crash upon the rocks so they can be plundered. He is in the watchtower but the storm will not abate and he cannot get a glimpse of the world. The storm has reached a crescendo and it rules. Every ship he has ever launched can sink, for all he cares. The art, his brewery, The Guild of St. Luke's, it can all go to Poseidon.

He shoots out of his "bed of nails" and runs full speed down the grand hallways. His ancestors smirk and glare at him like the sick monsters they probably were. He carries their curse. He will pass it on to the next generation, this curse of loneliness, lost love and obeying family rules that apply to a past that was a prisoner of itself. He must break the chains and move the planet forward. God gave man free will. Man took it away from himself. The constraints tie a man to him so he cannot choose. God's rules are so strict and society so stifled man cannot move in a new direction. But a new age is upon us and men like him will soon be enlightened.

The door to Maria's room is like a barrier to the truth. He kicks it in. His rage is so ripened from a night of torment he has the strength of a monster. He finds her standing in her robe glaring out into the endless pitch black of night that matches her heart and she still wears the earrings. He turns and like a zombie returns to his room where the portrait of Fleur only reminds him of his loss.

Chapter 44

Detective Vootenstrasse knows he soon must confront the painter. He is for now the number one suspect but the detective is certain he is not the culprit. However, if he had gone too far with the maiden his fears could have caused him to take action that may be regretful. Married men often get themselves into compromising situations. They lustfully and willfully make women with child and then dispense of them in an evil fashion in an attempt to disguise the disagreeable act.

The Guild of St. Luke's was meeting at the town hall today. He had read the poster announcing such an event. Vermeer was early as the detective surmised he would be. He observed the artist walking up the steps. He seemed to the detective to be in a faraway place. His expression was like that of a man who was very tired and needed a push to make it to the top. "Dear Fellow Vermeer!" The detective shouted out before he could enter the building. Vermeer was not certain the officer was speaking to him until he looked around and realized they were alone. "Yes, Officer Vootenstrasse, how is it I can be of assistance? If you have come regarding the benefit it will be..." "Oh no, no, no," the little man quickly went into the reason for approaching him. "I am here in the capacity of officer for the city of Delft to question you on an important matter regarding the disappearance of

Fleur Oster, the missing Mechelen maid." As always Vermeer remained silent for this was his nature. Quick responses and verbal jousting was not his cup of tea. Officer Vootenstrasse was a patient man. He could outwit and outwait most men as they searched around their heads for an answer that would not get them into trouble. "Oh yes it is a pity my mother is quite distraught. I do wish the police could solve this mystery for my mother's sake and the girl." The detective could sense the melancholy in his tone. Vermeer had always been reserved and quiet and these were the most words he had ever heard emitted from the artist.

"When was the last time you spoke to her? Your mother tells me she was a model for your recent portrait." Vermeer's mind raced. In a flash the episode of Fleur played out before his eyes. He knew he had to take control using all of his wits to protect his angel from any harm. If anyone were to discover the truth Maria would find her and this was out of the question.

Vermeer's dark eyes met the detectives in an effort to; ostensibly, demonstrate his honest nature and fearlessness. "Yes," he replied in his melancholy voice, "it was done very quickly, a rather informal piece. I really did so as a favor to my mother and the girl to improve their finances. The girl's duties at the Inn were many so she had little time to pose. It was not an important work.

The buyer has taken it out of the country. He has moved to the Spice Islands and desired a momentum of home. He longs to gaze upon a typical Dutch girl to remind him of Holland."

Too many words did not ring true but clanged and banged like a defective church bell. The man was shielding someone. He had proven himself an artist not an actor. But there was much drama surrounding this performance and the detective would soon drop the curtain on one of the players.

Chapter 45

The next morning Pieter took the painting of Fleur to the Mechelen. Digna hung it in clear view with a note asking for information that could lead to finding her. They should contact Officer Vootenstrasse directly. A substantial reward was offered by an anonymous, interested party.

Gertrude heard the men discussing the poster. She could not read or write so she listened intently to their comments. Fleur had started teaching her but she did not have enough time to learn. Here was her chance to get rich and go to jail at the same time. She could spill all the wine and Maria would be in trouble too. What a quagmire she was in, no one would believe her. She must go to Pieter. She must think greatly upon this matter. Her fear and skepticism of the upper class was like a lock to an ancient door. They stomped on her every day like she was a crumbled autumn leaf strewn on the neatly swept street. She had worked long days since she was a child. She feared she would soon lose her beauty and be mistaken for sixty at thirty, as her mother had.

Cook was slicing the oxen without a care for cutting off her fingers. Watching Gertrude she saw her guilt and her guts told her she was involved. She pounded the meat down to nothing. Gertrude had been very preoccupied since Fleur disappeared. Yet, there was nothing she could gain. Her work load had doubled and a good friend was lost. There was nothing in it for her on the surface. It was then Cook noticed someone had removed the broken panes from the storage room window where Vermeer had been working. Stuck on an old rusty nail was a piece of yellow ribbon. Immediately she recognized it as a piece of Gertrude's belt that she wore tightly around her waist. Looking like a lusty hourglass the men were happy to give her extra tips. Abandoning her meal preparation she gently lifted the ribbon, placed it in a pin box and ran to the police station, forgetting her shawl. There was a bottom to this and that is where they would find Fleur be she dead or alive.

Chapter 46

The splendor of Holland is never more vivid than in spring. A riot of tulips bloom in every color and urge the new season to shower the Dutch with beauty. Handcrafted buildings shine and decorate the roads and canals. It is hard to say if they are art or architecture. Couples walk along the trails hand in hand renewing love that has grown cold over a long and bitter winter. Life becomes easy again. Love's fever is out of control setting off the frenzy that keeps the population of Europe growing. It is expanding around the globe. The demand for human expansion has never been so urgent. Voltaire will be born in a few decades, in 1694. His philosophies and writings like "Candide" will stimulate a new generation to live with optimism. Self-reliance and personal independence will put religion on the backburner as a secular world takes the forefront. Exploration and greed will work hand in hand to achieve an end that in Vermeer's time was unimaginable. But men ahead of their day were roaming the seas and foreign lands to discover what everyone else was missing. They would bring back spices and tales that made the curious and troubled into sailors. It also gave people a chance to escape to a world where they would never be found.

Over one hundred and fifty years ago Magellan had circumvented the globe. One ship out of five, eleven men out of two hundred and sixty-eight limped back to Spain with rigging rotted off the ship and no leader. He had been consumed not only by the voyage but angry natives as well. They despised his warlike manners and missionary bullying. They loved their gods so much they sacrificed the explorer and then ate him for good measure. America was in its infancy. Risk takers and escapees were attracted to its shore and dreams of a better world were being formed. Those returning with tales of riches and freedom dazzled a society that was stifled from centuries of oppression.

Chapter 47

Detective Vootenstrasse was shocked to see the picture of Fleur, her innocent face beaming above him. Vermeer had mentioned it was on its way to the Spice Islands. He would soon be back to question him or take him in. For the moment he would root around some more. Something or someone was sticking in his craw. He did not like the sound of this Maria Van Ruijven who brought Gertrude to the Inn in such a timely manner. She was next to question. Gertrude and Maria, they were the ones on his mind. Cook had brought him the yellow ribbon following his orders not to leave a thread behind. It was interesting that it matched the belt the lusty tavern maiden wore. Was it important? He could not yet be sure. But the windmill, the portrait and the ribbon all tied together. The web was being spun. Soon it would trap his fly.

Chapter 48

Gertrude was now sleeping in Fleur's bed. It was the most comfortable she had ever slept in, but it was not comforting. She lay awake, her mind like an ocean whose waves rolled over and over a ship in great peril. The detective had spent much time today asking her a lot of questions about Fleur. He was not so funny close up. There was something creepy and unearthly about him. He looked like he crawled out from under a rock. She was surprised there was no mold to be found on his badge. Beady blue eyes were practically covered by his bushy eyebrows. His unruly nose hairs were grey and unsightly. Not once did he look at her overflowing bosom. Instead he looked her right in the eye making her uneasy. Men never looked at her face. Her breasts, her only defense, were of little value to the odd little man. Defenseless, her answers stumbled out of her mouth like drunken men out of the Mechelen's door. The questions kept coming like arrows attacking a castle about to surrender. She could not say where Fleur had gone. She did mention an aunt in London. Her parents and grandparents were dead. Yes, she seemed to enjoy sitting for the painting. Yes, she liked working at the Inn. No, she had not one enemy.

When he finally left Gertrude was spent. Digna gave her the afternoon off and she tossed in bed unable to halt the thoughts that were tormenting her every waking hour. But her fears and the reward were starting to work together and make sense. That was scarier than the detective. She must gather her strength to approach Pieter. Perhaps then he would help abate this nightmare and happily give her the reward that would free her of herself.

Chapter 49

Maria was caught off guard by the detective's visit. He pretended he was there to do a background check on Gertrude. He would ask Maria if she was of good character. While employed was she honest and faithful. Did she ever display behavior that leads Maria to believe she could hurt Fleur?

Maria saw the little munchkin of a man ascending her numerous front steps. She was appalled at his appearance. To her he looked like an unwelcome spider. Dressed in black and hairy everywhere she thought she would rather dine with an arachnid.

When Officer Vootenstrasse entered the parlor Maria was seated at her embroidery table not looking the least bit cordial. The two did not speak at first. He was overwhelmed by the opulence of the house. The amount of wealth surrounding him was staggering. What could anyone in this mansion gain from hurting Fleur? Then he remembered the dark man whose eyes followed Fleur around the Inn. It was Pieter Van Ruijven and this woman before him, seated in such grandeur, was his wife. The diary had many times alluded to Pieter. They seemed to have a very agreeable relationship. It did not appear romantic in any sense. It was the artist she yearned for. Every entry brought her closer to Vermeer.

Sometimes she would close with a scribbled poem that came from the depths of a girl too much in love with a man that was beyond her reach. However, she never divulged any information that led the officer to believer Vermeer had responded to her steamy passion.

Unfortunately, getting cooperation from Maria was like attempting to remove a bone from the jaws of an angry pit bull. She acted like the spoiled and apathetic citizen she was. How dare he question her on this matter. She had nothing to do with lowly Gertrude. Since she brought her to the Mechelen her existence was forgotten. How dare he come to her and speak on matters that concerned the lower class. She could not help. Tugging on the butler's rope she wanted him led away so she could forget his ugliness. Officer Vootenstrasse bowed and said his farewell adding he hoped she would contact him if she thought of anything that could assist the police.

Maria was annoyed when he did not depart immediately. Instead he turned to the mantle and commented on the porcelain shoe. "It is so much like Digna's windmill at the Mechelen. Is it perhaps crafted by the same tradesman? My wife is always wishing for such trinkets to decorate her little hutch. Alas, not on a detective's wages." Maria froze and stopped in her tracks momentarily. She stomped her foot in annoyance. "Detective, I asked you to leave, not to do a dissertation on my art collection. I will contact your supervisors and ask them to have you removed from office. Do not return if you value your job or citizenship in Delft."

Once outside the spring air cleared his stuffed up head. Removing his hat he scratched his head in annoyance and shame. He had a hard time concentrating on that session. For the entire interview was spent analyzing the earrings that hung on her flabby earlobes. He was certain they were identical to the ones Fleur wore in the portrait.

Back at his work desk he spent an hour sketching Maria's cartoon face wearing the pearl earrings. She was an ugly woman and he thought she looked much like an anteater. His rendition when finished had an evil aura about it. He was closing in and the show would soon end for Vermeer, Maria or Pieter. He could smell an arrest when his nose started jerking around like a rabbit. He had to pinch it to make it stop or everyone in the precinct would know the case would soon be closed.

Chapter 50

"Once again, where did you get the earrings?" Pieter pushed his wife against the wall of her room with no mercy. She felt like a doll made out of straw. She was so emaciated her bones were more prevalent than her flesh. But this did not diminish her resolve to make his misery last for the rest of his life. "I told you I bought these on our last trip to Paris at the little jewelers on the Rue Des Palais. He was very clever at crafting paste into pearls." Pieter's anger was heightened to where he could feel his heart was about to burst out of his silk vest, but he continued to scream. "Liar, you know they are Fleur's. You have robbed them from her and her from me. Give them to me you ancient hag and you will tell me where she can be found." Maria's face laughed and cracked at the same time. "You are a fool Pieter. I assure you I know of no one by that dreadful name. These earrings are mine and I will call the police if you handle me again." Suddenly Pieter calmed himself and took several steps backward. "That would be a jolly good idea; I shall be on my way to fetch Officer Vootenstrasse."

Pieter was relieved to have been called away from Delft on an urgent business matter. The maid had packed a few of his essentials and he was off in his newly renovated carriage. The thick velvet felt like a warm hug and assuaged the pain that never abated. It was a perfect day with a sky that could not be duplicated on any canvas. The clouds looked as welcoming as a down comforter and the blue that surrounded them reminded him of Tessa's eyes. Soon, my love, I will find our daughter. This I owe you and her. It will be small compensation for how I abandoned you and the life I long for. Once my head is in control of thought I will return and seek out Officer Vootenstrasse and the truth.

Chapter 51

During Officer Vootenstrasse's final questioning of Gertrude he wore her down to pulp. The tell tale heart surrendered. The story spewed out of her mouth like the foam of a wave that crashed against rocks waiting patiently for the impact.

She was told to reveal nothing to another soul. He would seek clemency for her if and when arrests were made. For now she should continue her duties uninterrupted. He asked her to stay in Delft and remain available to him at all times. Unfortunately, he was convinced the girl was clueless as to Fleur's whereabouts. He sensed she missed her tavern friend and had convinced him she was loath to do Maria's dirty work.

The world was an unfair place. He had seen the wealthy walk away from the gallows after depositing large sums into the coffers of higher up henchmen. The poor had not a chance. Stealing a loaf of bread could send them to prison for years. There was no balance. Justice was blindfolded with guilders and political promises. That had never been his concern until now. Gertrude was the lamb and Maria was the wolf that society would let loose to pounce upon an innocent. Her money and power worked together to maneuver around the law like the worst of criminals. The artist they would prosecute to the fullest extent of the law. His body would hang from a rope with little effect except upon the poor street children who would come to stare and throw rotten things at the corpse. However, Maria would be absolved by a court system as corrupt as a marauding pack of bandits.

He now had the ammunition but he would delay the firing of the weapon. His desk back at his humble cottage was a good place to be. It was like an old friend whose conversation gave him insight. His mind slowed down a bit and the wheels started to turn in a different direction.

His wife brought the piping bowl of hot water into his study. He took off his old striped sock that smelled badly and needed darning. His big toe had been sticking out and he could see the toenail curling and cracked. This was the suspect that had caused him to hobble home. The steamy water sizzled when he finally soaked himself. He let his mind wander and almost went off duty. Alandra would soon come back to clip his toes and wrap them up nice and tidy. She would first apply a balm that was from a secret family recipe of special healing herbs and such. His feet were an important part of any investigation as critical as his brain. When he calculated the amount of miles he traveled in his journey to right all of the wrongs he understood why the calluses on his feet were so thick. Soon he would put them and his feet to rest.

He took out Fleur's diary and laid it before him. Tonight he would not read any entries. It was her private place and he felt like he had invaded it. Of course, before he had solved the mystery it was unavoidable. Never again would he intrude on her private thoughts and desires. Everyone had a right to seek their own philosophy and life path. As long as they were obeying the law there was no problem. These were, in reality a conscious agreement of the people. Ancient Greece and Rome passed down these basic principals which brought us out of the Dark Ages. Yet, times are changing as fast as the daffodils nod their bonnets during a windstorm. Society was not going backwards. These were pivotal times. Columbus had proven over a century past that the planet was not flat. There is no longer an excuse to fall off. Humanity has gone around the globe and must now free itself to explore the truth.

Chapter 52

Magdalena was waiting for her father when he arrived home from his business trip. She was very serene and looked almost pretty in her comfortable daisy housedress. When she wore her hair in braids Pieter remembered she was also his little girl. He felt a pang of guilt at having ignored her over the years. He had never seen such determination in her dark blue eyes. Today they seemed a shade darker like an artist had added a dab of black to the ultramarine. He was still wearing his cloak when those eyes met with his, "Mother is gone, and she took all of your guilders, family jewels and the finest paintings. She tried to force me to join her on the ship 'Wander' before setting sail. I could not leave you Father no matter you love Fleur more than me. I understand how you must have felt losing your true love for I know how I feel when I think you really do not love me."

Pieter was at a loss for words. He took his daughter in his arms holding her for a moment". I am pleased you are staying with me child. Perhaps you will not grow into a replica of your mother after all. We will christen this day as the vessel that will send our relationship off on a new journey. You are quite a bright student and talented musician. Perhaps I can make an effort to help you achieve any goals you seek in those areas. Magdalena, I want to love you, please help me."

Magdalena broke away and helped her father remove his dusty travel cloak. Although it was rugged it still boasted the finest material and trimmings. She bid him to sit in his favorite chair of leather. When it was empty she yearned for him to just be home by the fire. "Father, I have been spying on mother for months. I was fully aware of her diabolical plot. Yesterday, I walked all the way to Mechelen. Oh yes, you look surprised at my resolve. Fear not, I have some of my mother's strengths and your determination within me. I approached Gertrude and she was full of horror at the sight of me. I brought her to the park and it was such a lovely day, so in contrast to the ugly tale she told filling in all the missing gaps for me. It was too much for her and she was quite shook up. Officer Vootenstrasse had just left and I believe he had gathered critical information from her. She was as shaken as a rabbit forced out of its hole by a wiley predator. I quickly returned home and told Mother how Gertrude had bludgeoned Fleur to death sending her to a watery grave. I went on to tell her that she had confided in me that the detective was hot on the trail. Everything would soon be out in the open. Gertrude was at her breaking point. Finally, I set the trap reporting they had found the body and all was certainly lost. I lied father, it is not true. Gertrude is not capable of such foul play. I regret treating her so miserably. Perhaps I was jealous of her comely looks and shapely physique. Father, you must believe me, she let Fleur go! She took the earrings so Mother would believe your daughter dead and this I let her believe. Fearing arrest and the wrath of Detective Vootenstrasse she has escaped to her brother's expansive plantation in Virginia. She would like me to follow someday. I promised I would after Frederick and I are married, another lie. I begged her to loan me the earrings so I may wear them on my wedding day." With this she opened her palm and revealed the pearl earrings. They looked so innocent in Magdalena's finely formed hand. Her long tapered fingers looked beautiful holding them for they were her finest features. Pieter looked astounded and was frozen in time. "Father I want to help you find Fleur for she is also my sister and I have always longed for one."

Pieter finally awakened to the truth that brought such relief. His emotions were bouncing around like a ship tossed about in a sea where the gusts come and go, confusing the captain and crew until the sails luff and the rigging must once again be reset to catch the wind. "Yes, Daughter let us begin this hardship together for there is strength in a common cause."

Pieter rose from his chair and put his arm around Magdalena's waist. They walked together to the oversized window that looked out upon Delft. Silently they looked upon their world. It was a scene they knew so well. Yet, it was as if they were viewing it for the first time, bathed in a light that only the sun god could bestow. They both were amazed that Fleur was out there beyond the windmills and canals waiting for them. Their positive energy could be felt throughout the house that was now at last, a home.

Chapter 54

The detective watched the "Wanderer" leave port with much pleasure. Arrest would have been as easy as gulping down his favorite ale. Yet, he let her slink up the plank to the sanctuary of the cabins below deck. He was so close he could hear her little pups yapping at all the unfamiliar activity of a vessel about to disembark. With so much baggage he was certain the ship would sink and not even the sharks would find a meal on Maria's bones. He could not bring himself to take her in. It would certainly cause a domino effect of problems. Ultimately, he feared his superiors would find a loophole for the rich and she would remain in Delft making everyone miserable forever.

Maria had finally caught herself up in a web she so intricately crafted. The innocents she had set out to destroy were now free of her poisonous fangs. She had done an excellent job at attempting to ruin lives of citizens who were leading society away from crime and injustice. Worst of all if the corrupt courts released Maria on some unforeseen technicality Fleur would be in danger again.

He felt good about his dereliction of duty. Never before had he allowed a suspect to flee so willingly. The time had come for him to retire. This would be his last case. He will leave one unsolved. This way the young officers can feel they can excel in their own careers. They will believe they have a chance to better old Detective Vootenstrasse's record.

He was really thirsty now. There was nothing he sought more at this precise moment than a beer stein filled to the brim with a cold dark brew. His instinct would lead him to the closest local tavern. There he would do nothing but observe the colors of the various ales and partake of many. The sailors had all left the wharf. They had taken their leave passes and were off in search of lusty Dutch girls who would offer them a warm bed. It would help them forget the perils of the ocean and its unimaginable depth. The only sound was the creaking of the small ships struggling with the ropes that were keeping them prisoner at the port. Farther out in the bay several catches were still anchored down waiting for the stars that would help them navigate their course to the new world. The water was like glass, giving the unlucky crew left behind to keep watch a safe haven.

The sun was setting now. He could see it settling on the horizon, bathing itself in the welcoming sea. It was almost dark and somehow this was comforting. He was entering the dusk of his life and he had no fear. Old age would provide greater wisdom and death the ultimate truth. He closed his eyes for a moment and he could hear the ocean gently consenting to the choice he made. In the morning he would return to Delft and this night would be a just a memory, like so many others.

He looked out at the expanse of water and sky that led to the new world, certain there was so much he would never know. He had spent a lifetime seeking the truth and knowledge grew like the branches of an oak tree until the rain bent down the bough of an old man, crooked and tired. The detective pulled his well-worn cap over his exposed ears and scratched his long pointy nose with a quick swipe. Suddenly, as if duty called, he turned away and never looked back.

Epilogue- Eight Years Later

Catarina stood by their bed holding her dead husband's cape. She thought of all the love, children and comfort they had achieved over a lifetime of commitment, and unfortunately, the debt.

She had to sell everything. His clothing, paints, brushes and canvasses. Every last painting had gone quickly to greedy buyers who took advantage of her poverty and sudden widowhood. But this she would keep. It was all she had of him, so warm and manly. It was not a refined piece of clothing for he loved rugged attire, yet he had weaknesses that allowed his world to kill him. She smiled when she inhaled, for certain the smell of linseed oil and musky soap still lingered in his garment.

As she held it closer she thought she heard a crackling. Curious, she felt deep inside his cloak's inner pocket, where a piece of sketch paper was secured with a small pin. Her nimble fingers carefully released it so she could look upon it. Her heart started pounding so loudly she thought it might burst. There, like a woman fresh in love, was Fleur. He had sketched her in great detail. It was almost more dramatic than the painting in its simplicity. The corners were frayed and yellow, but her face was as beautiful as the rising sun, triumphant in its youth and splendor. When she turned it around her breath came like the sharp sound of a knife trying to cut ice.

For it read: "My Golden Angel."

THE ROUGH WOOING

Chapter 1

Lord Bothwell drove his stallion galloping over the rugged Scottish terrain. He appeared to have been born and bred an equestrian. The animal seemed attached and in full concert with his master. Neither feared the impending storm as the wind lashed mercilessly like an ancient banshee. Handsome, assertive and always the aristocrat, men wished to align themselves to his causes or kill him. Women could not say no as they opened their legs and coffers. Yet, he did not feel the strength he had under Marie of Guise's rule. She had been the wife of James V. Following his death their infant Mary became the anointed Queen of Scotland. Marie was regent and Bothwell had used all of his political finesse and power to guide her through the labyrinth the lords of the Protestant Congregation were planting. They were hoping to thwart the Catholic dowager queen and her devout daughter. For over one hundred years all Scottish monarchs inherited the throne in their childhood. As a result, the nobility became powerful. Factions chafed against one another and fires were lit that could not be doused by any queen. One lord would become the head of the octopus. The others were his tentacles, sent far and wide to grab all of the power that they could wield. There was a constant tug of war between the rivals who had little concern for the monarchy. Impacting the lords was the rise of Protestantism and their ability to have Parliament deem it the true and legal religion of Scotland. The cauldron boiled across continents and seas until the whirlpool of religious opposition ripped countries up by their roots. This new religion bloomed with the return of John Knox. He had come out of exile, gloriously returned to Scotland a hero and leader of the Reformation in Scotland. His influence would play a critical role and turn the pages of history.

Marie of Guise had sent her daughter to France as a child, promised to The Dauphine Francis. Her intentions were multiple. She wanted her raised a Catholic. She would be an anointed queen of Scotland, France and yes England. This would strengthen Scotland's and France's alliance against England. But most importantly, she feared Henry VIII. He was invading Scotland in order to force Mary to marry his son Edward. The marriage that would have solidified Henry's ideal of a perfect succession never took place. Now, Henry was dead. All of the terror he bestowed on the northlands failed. The Rough Wooing is the name historians assign to this conflict. It was the last major war before 1603 with the Union of the Crowns. The Scots called it the Nine Years' War since Henry had a hard time giving up. He was a spoiled and aggressive king who lopped off his wives heads and invaded France and Scotland like he was taking tea.

The snow was mounting now as the horse struggled against the coastal winds. Bothwell thought how unfortunate it was that James V had died at the Battle of Solway Moss. He left behind the infant Mary and a wife that could not control the lords whose Protestant grasp could bend a crucifix in half. Although his fingers were frozen, he grasped the reins like he was on holiday. Inside he was as warm as the queen's fur lined garments. A fire burned there that he never should have lit. He had loved Mary Queen of Scots at first sight. What man could not? She was six feet tall yet slender and well built, rising above the average 5'5" man. Her features were so well formed they told a story. A longish Stuart nose should have disturbed, but instead enhanced. Beautiful and charismatic, even as a child she dumbfounded the King of France. He had been enthralled and adored the newly arrived princess. She was art to his French court. Yet, she had grown into a rugged and skilled horsewoman who could lead a cavalry into battle. Hawking was as important to her as embroidery. She excelled in both. Her southern cousin Queen Elizabeth was frustrated at her uncontested beauty. It was a small dagger stuck in her gut like a raw potato that could not find a way out. William Cecil, Elizabeth's secretary and closest advisor had to dance around all issues pertaining to Mary. Her Majesty became quite red at the mention of her lovelier relative. He needed to reassure her over and over that her own unique beauty was not eclipsed. Sometimes she would slap him if he or anyone mentioned the fame of Mary's beauty in her presence. Regardless of

Cecil's distain for Mary and the unruly Scots he wanted Elizabeth to crush and control.

Yes, Bothwell's love, Mary, was the envy of Europe. Her royal carriage and physical pleasantries intrigued society. She was a living legend. Artists clamored for a commission to paint her. He held her in esteem above all worldly possessions. His greatest desire was to gaze upon her countenance. She stopped his heart from beating. How odd that she had started it beating. Taken for dead after a serious hunting accident his entourage had returned him to Hermitage Castle expecting a burial. Upon hearing this news Mary drove her horse sixty miles through storms and dangerous terrain to be by his side. That is when he knew he had captured her love. To this day he bore the scar on his forehead sustained from that injury. It was a tattoo of love that he wore with great affection as a constant reminder of their love. Soon all would be revealed as this. If all went as planned the poor excuse for a king, Darnley, would be dead. They would marry and rule together. His Protestant faith and her Catholic devotion combined would show Scotland that the country could live in peace regardless of a subject's religious beliefs. Scotland would bow to them. Theirs would be an egalitarian rule. Her voice would be his. He thought of all the languages she had perfected. Fluent in French, she could discuss court politics in the gardens of Versailles. She was also a brave soldier. A mathematician and women of logic, she had read all of the Greeks and could translate Homer if asked. With natural acumen for military tactics she could draw up a battle plan. Still, she was the loveliest wave on a calm sea lulling you into a trance. But, he had seen the stormy side of her. The hatred she bore for Darnley. How she detested that man. Then he had felt the passion in their lovemaking. What a whore she could be at the same time as he worshiped her. Shocked and excited by her aggressive bed manners he climaxed as if for the first time, every time. Her slender white fingers were taken from oriental paintings he had seen on his travels to Italy. Marco Polo had started a craze. There was talk of sexual delights hidden in these portraits. Her fingers caressed his reed like those women stroked their odd instruments. The French court was permissive by staunch Scottish standards. Mary had grown up uninhibited regarding matters of sex. In bed she was no longer Mary Queen of Scots. She was his alone.

Chapter 2

Lord Darnley sat naked on the bed with his Master of the Horse. He was rubbing Ian's hair with gentle circular motions. The love making had gone on endlessly. It never ceased to amaze him how he could hold on for a man. Yet, with the queen he could not remain alert but for a fleeting moment. How he had produced enough seed within her to father the future King of Scotland was something he could not grasp. Flopping down he pulled out his favorite snuff box making vulgar sounds as he inhaled the addictive fragrance. Why was his mind like a pet monkey? It kept coming back to his problems with that wretched queen of his. It could not keep still. Killing her closest friend and advisor was not enough. He had despised David Rizzo. All of the lords had their fill of him. She would take advice from none but that loathsome creature. He was an aristocratic Italian she had met in France. He had cast a spell over her years ago. If you wanted her audience you had to get his approval, and it was a process. She was lucky they did not kill her and she knew it. That is why she had run off to Bothwell for protection. But now all of the lords including her stepbrother, The Earl of Moray, had been forgiven and returned from exile in England. How lucky he had been that she believed he had been innocent, when he had indeed hatched the plot. Yes, the lords had conspired with him and fueled his anger and resolve, but he was the guiltiest of all. What a fool.

But what could she do. I am the father of the heir apparent and my blood is royal and our heritage closely shared. He laughed out loud when he thought of the look on her face as the dagger was driven into Rizzo over and over in her very presence. At Mary's dinner table in her private closet the sacrifice was eagerly performed. The lords were the high priests who bargained with higher powers to achieve their ends. No cost was too great. Why does she not give up? Take mass in private. Let them have the power they seek. Either they rule or I should finally be awarded the crown matrimonial. Which will it be? But she is relentless in her quest to defy them and me her lawful husband and king.

It would be best if she would agree with me. We could just wallow in the glory and benefits that belong to those with royal blood. Alas! She will never be like me, agree with me or most importantly ever touch me again. Her demise is in the stars. My soothsayer has mapped out her destruction and, unless the moon falls out of the sky, the thorn will soon be out of my side.

I begged her not to allow the return of her evil brother. He will seek revenge upon me for playing the innocent. I can feel the hatred of the lords as they look upon me. Neither are they fond of her. This is a recipe for disaster. We will be brought down and fall like upon jagged rocks.

Without another thought he crawled back under his down cover that boasted the Lennox crest. Darnley was proud that he was so close to the throne of England and Scotland. With enough machinations he may one day have a successful conspiracy and rule both lands. Ian was sound asleep but Darnley was a rude and uncaring lover. He pulled his hair and shoved the poor lad under the covers like he wanted him drowned. This is where he wanted to see his subjects and below them Mary would be in her place where she belonged.

Chapter 3

Wemyss Castle stood above the sea, a great defense against the surge of Scotland's enemies. How it was built defies gravity and nature. Hundreds of mules and men toiled to raise her up from the sea to protect their homeland. The realm boasted many castles and lords and ladies all who held claims of royalty or connections thereof. Many lords had gotten their fists tightly around at least one fortress while Marie of Guise fought a losing battle. The most powerful of these, the Earl of Moray, was at the head of these men. He was Mary's illegitimate stepbrother. They shared the same father, but were nothing alike. He was quiet but forceful. Words came parceled out with care, but if you crossed him he would have you burned at the stake in an instant with little thought. But mostly, he hated Catholics. He knew his sister was the one who should burn and soon he would have his way and rule, guardian to his nephew James VI. The infant was under the auspices of the lords and would soon be swept safely away from his Pope loving mother. He would be king and a Protestant one at that. It was destined and imperative so Queen Elizabeth would have no objection to choosing him as her heir.

Last night the lords had met in the great hall. It was so cold beyond the stone walls your breath might freeze. Pewter wine goblets were everywhere.

The brainstorming had gone on so late that plates filled with half chewed bones lingered waiting for the cock to crow awakening the servants. The men were gearing up to oust that papist slip of a girl. Why had he not been born to Marie of Guise? The male succession was so necessary to carry on a strong line and tight fisted rule. Women were weak by nature; therefore, they could not perform the duties of a monarch. What a twist of fate. It goes in like a dagger a little deeper each day. But now he had the proof they were planning on killing Darnley. He was so glad they would beat him to the act. That rat had been in on the plot to kill Rizzo and lied to the queen about his involvement. Meanwhile, he was exiled to England where he had to bow low to Elizabeth and grovel before her hoping to remain in her favor. Fortunately, she saw the advantage of protecting him from Mary. He would be a useful ally and spy, for she could see he was a master. Now that Mary had called him back to the fold everything seemed reconciled on the surface, but a poisonous brew was bubbling underneath. Soon Mary would be forced to drink her own concoction destroying herself.

This would be the final straw. Yesterday he watched her work her skillful hands across tapestry. She was fashioning the Stuart motto upon it. IN MY END IS MY BEGINNING. Alas! This will be her end. He looked up and caught his reflection in the mirror that was illuminating in the frigid room. He thought he saw the devil.

Chapter 4

When one thinks of a Protestant whose voice rose above all others, John Knox is not far behind Martin Luther and his mentor Calvin. He sat before the fire in his comfortable castle that the lords had awarded him on his return to the realm from exile. As he gazed into the fire you could see him forging metal in his mind. His thought hissed and burned as he continued his plan to wipe Catholicism off the face of Scotland. It actually made him ill to think they believed in the transmutation of the host. No man could turn bread into God. Only God had such powers. Worshipping statues of Mother Mary was vulgar. It was no different than the Israelites worshipping the golden calf while God was etching the Ten Commandments on stone for Moses.

He had blessed the lords and was ready to guide the infant James VI. He would be the first generation to be raised from infancy in the true Protestant religion. He will learn the meaning of Jesus's teaching and his kingdom will double. He was certain the lords had amassed an abundance of power and would soon rule this unruly land. Many of the subjects needed taming and only the Bible would save their savage souls. Queen Mary was such a frivolous ruler. She lacked tact and could not manage a group of troubadours. She flaunts her blasphemous religion and calls on other kings of her faith to help her reinstate the Pope's rule. She was responsible for the death of Rizzo, provoking the lords into murdering him when she failed time and time again to take their sound advice. He had been privy to the plan and blessed the entire episode. Had she not fled to Bothwell her assassination may have followed.

He sat back in his chair and drew in a long breath. The icicles hung outside his window like spirits of the night. If you were to look through that window you would be surprised to see a slight person with a tight cap and very long grey beard. His beady blue eyes belied a highly intelligent man who could read the Bible at four years old. The people must follow the kingdom of our Lord. Like sheep they must be protected from the wolf. The very soul of this nation is hinging on the abdication of this whore of Babylon. From the pulpit he had openly called her a Jezebel and would not rescind. It was published for all to read and he would not take back a syllable. His message was clear, Mary was unfit to rule. She had crawled out of her French hole returning to poison his flock. Why did she not remain with those fish eating French blasphemers? That country was so corrupt and filthy and she fit the mold. We want none of their man made doctrines and ostentatious cathedrals. Catholics were not following Christ's teachings. They were practicing a life that directly opposed his word. Faith was the cornerstone, the gist of his command.

Good deed doers would burn in hell without faith. Yet they boast of their works, against God's word. He thought back to when he had been ministering to King Edward, Henry's son. Unfortunately, upon his death that vixen Mary I, brought back her papist religion and he had to flee from England as he had from Scotland. At least her Sister Elizabeth had good sense. She was forced to choose between The Tower of London, or going to Mass. She pretended in Protestant beliefs, bidding her time like a cunning ruler would until the devil welcomed her evil sister. Mary's rule was mercifully short, yet, hundreds burned at the stake for not attending Mass.

The pain in his hands continued to plague him. He had severe arthritis from rowing as a galley slave. He would ignore the pain. Not once did he regret his involvement in the plot to kill Cardinal Beaton. How dare he have burned a Protestant reformer at the stake? This discomfort was nothing compared to what Jesus endured on the cross. He had walked with the cross on his back releasing us from the burden of original sin. His death would free us. He, John Knox, was also on a journey to show mortal men the road to salvation. He must crucify himself, but someone had to drive the last nail through his hand. Jesus had saved us as he must save Scotland. The lords held that last nail, and he would urge them to complete the task. Mary, what blasphemy she has given that name. Surely she worships herself as she kneels in front of the mother of God at prayer.

Chapter 5

How naïve she had been to think that her brother, the Earl of Moray, would align himself with a Catholic queen. Blood was not thicker than water with this bastard. It boiled and smelled fetid like a foul stream. He was lucky she had called him back from exile after he had a hand in Rizzo's murder. Now he had all of his lands back and the rebel lords flocked to him like old crows planning to devour a wounded deer.

The rain was perpetual. Mary picked up her brush and found the energy for one hundred strokes. Although the mirror showed a face of chiseled beauty and aristocratic skin, she felt ancient. As her mind was wondering off, Mary Beaton, one of the faithful four Maries abruptly entered the room, James VI, the heir apparent in her arms. She shivered when she thought of how grueling the labor had been. She would like to see the lords endure such torture to provide their country with a king.

It was her appointed time for Mother to show interest in the everyday needs of a baby. Not just any baby, the future King of Scotland and England. She was the rightful heir as was he. Never would she sign the Act of Succession that awful Henry had enacted and forced the masses to endorse. First her head would roll and topple over

Elizabeth. She shouted to the world, to anyone who would listen that she was the true Queen of England. She was the closest legitimate living relative of Henry VIII. Her grandmother was his sister who married a Scottish king to please her father, the taciturn Henry VII. Elizabeth was Ann Boleyn's bastard. There was no allowance for the succession of offspring of the king's whores. If there were, heads would roll each day and the Tower of London would be bursting at the seams. Henry had created a dilemma that spanned generations when he disobeyed the Pope who would not grant him a divorce from Katherine of Aragon.

Mary held the boy who seemed in a serene state for a change. He really was not attractive. Even as a mother she could not deny he was skinny and puny. He would not be handsome this was clear. This struck her as odd since her and Darnley were revered for their physical pleasantries. The Lord worked in strange ways. None the less, he must acquire traits that will make him a great ruler. Scotland is a merciless land surrounded by wild seas and Englishmen.

Time passed. She could see the sun slipping away without care. Wherever did it go leaving darkness behind? If she could command it like her subjects it would bow and keep her safe in perpetual light. Bothwell was like that, always there for her. He was the orb that shone so brightly in her life. His energy and devotion was seemingly boundless. Once she possessed him, there was no turning back the Elizabethan clock. Why had she defied her cousin Elizabeth and married Darnley. She would be now free. Elizabeth was fearful of their combined heritage. As a Lennox he was arguably close to the throne. Margaret Tudor, Henry VIII's sister was their shared grandmother. There was no denying his Tudor heritage. Due to his father being exiled in England his birth there further enhanced his claim. However, his lineage was watered down. His mother, The Countess of Lennox was a product of their grandmother's second marriage following the Scottish king's death. Unfortunately for Darnley, unlike Mary's father, Archibald Douglas the sixth Earl of Angus was no king. Darnley had insisted many times that he should like to usurp the present monarch of England. She shook her head as she remembered the Lennox motto he had forced her to embroider. It read "Who hopes still constantly with patience shall at last obtain victory." Her cousin Elizabeth must view this as treasonous. It is no wonder Lady Lennox's second home is the tower. It had been rumored Darnley had a following in Scotland and Ireland that were conspiring at this very moment. They were all cousins. England had a long history of royal cousins who despised each other. The war of the roses had ended but not the rivalry. She thought for a moment of how she and Elizabeth would never meet. Mary had dreamt many times of failed rendezvous. They would continue to throw daggers across the border hoping they would hit the target ending a struggle that began with royal birth and death.

Well here is royalty that emerged from my loins the undisputed heir. I carried him for the Crown and delivered him to this island. Like me he is placed between God and man. He will be anointed with sacred oil and live his life above all of his subjects on earth. God guides him; therefore, his word is holy and pure. How sad I am that soon I must surrender him to my subjects and he shall no longer belong to me.

I know what Bothwell and I have planned are in his best interests. His father will be his ruination. Sons so like to imitate their father, especially when they are kings. I will not have him hear of Darnley carousing with prostitutes. He is constantly drunk. He cares only for hunting and hawking when he is sober. My child will witness his lazy ways and inability to rule. Worst of all he has contracted the French disease. This will further erode his mind and his physical person.

The rain still pounded Holyrood House. She thought of how their plot was unfolding and history was driving them forward like the cavalry rushed toward the enemy in the heat of battle. She could only pray for their success. This place was such a comfortable home and she intended on living here for years. For generations the Stuarts added portraits of their loved ones to adorn the walls. Now her portrait hung in all its glory above the fireplace whose flames enhanced her every feature and jeweled crown. How warm little James VI was like her own little belly hearth. He gurgled and kicked his feet about in complete contentment. His fingers went round hers and he looked up with adoring trust. If she could suspend time and take control of each and every moment, she would sit here forever. But, she had no choice and was forced to relent to the hourglass that was spewing sand through the tiny channel giving birth to each second without fail.

Chapter 6

The Catholic lords were now in the minority. Their power was dwindling like a snow pile that melts when the temperature rises above freezing. Some were feigning belief in the Protestant religion in order to save their hides. Families were divided all over Scotland, England and Europe. But Scotland was by heritage a feuding land. The lack of a strong monarch, the ongoing border disputes, remote castles and lords that sucked the life out of weak rulers were breeding grounds for the Reformation from hell. Mary thought about her own dilemma as she rode to Kirk o' Fields just outside of Edinburgh. Pope Pius V was constantly sending her directives. He had even suggested she prompt Phillip II of Spain to assist her in reinstating the true church of God to the Scottish people through force. Her Guise uncles in France were devout Catholic and would advise their king to join forces in the holy cause. However, she realized Parliament would never rescind the act that deemed Protestantism the supreme state religion. Also, her obsession with the English succession was eclipsing almost all other matters in her life. She often looked back on the Rough Wooing and lamented that her Great Uncle Henry had not seized her. Or, perhaps if her mother had not been tormented by him she would have remained in her domain. Mayhap she could have influenced her subjects and parliament to keep the faith of their fathers. Instead her first language was French. Her manners were as refined and cultured as any monarch on the Continent. She was anointed a queen twice in the true faith at Sterling Castle here and in France. With pomp and splendor the French Dauphine Francis and his fairy tale queen were dressed in gold and surrounded by magnificence as they were married in Notre-Dame. They were on top of the world above all mortals. Though gentle Francis was sickly and full of eczema he glowed that day. How could they have known how soon they would rule and he would die. His grandfather, always unaware of his mortality, was killed in a jousting accident. The chain of events made her an anointed queen twice over by the age of seventeen. Her life had been doubly blessed. It was filled with admirers and Guise Uncles who adored her. She was the jewel that would place the family in the palm of the French Court. Their influence would rise in direct proportion with their fortune. She was pampered and loved by all. Unfortunately, her return to Scotland had thrown her into a den of lions. They would devour her and savor the crunching of her delicate bones. She was not free to worship. Mass was a secret ceremony. Worst of all they had killed David Rizzo her closest friend and advisor in her presence. Of course, Darnley had been at the root of it, though she had been forced to turn her head. He would remain by her side while the others were exiled. When they were forgiven he had begged her to add a condition that they remain outside of Edinburgh for two years. He understood the danger the rebel lords meant for him. The fool should realize that his greatest enemy lay in his bed. She would kill him while he slept with her bejeweled dagger and bathe in his blood.

February was a month she would command to have removed from the calendar. The ride from Holyrood house to Kirk o' Fields was short but the mud and ice made it an unpleasant one. Any attempt to see her husband was most unwelcomed. She had tried to do the right thing. Darnley's blood was royal, he was Catholic. He had youth and a degree of intelligence. When they met she had been moved by his good looks and athletic interests. They both loved hawking and hunting. He could ride with her for hours showing her his love and ability with equine. She had conceived his son, the heir, healthy and ripe for throne of Scotland and England. It did not take more than three months for her to realize the folly of the union. He had been spoiled by his Lennox parents who filled his head with false hopes for ascension. He could not button his own riding jacket. His doublet was constantly stained with wine and food was rubbed in as he slept off a constant hangover. He brooded day in and out for she had postponed awarding him the crown matrimonial until the distant future. Never could she agree to his right to co-reign with her. He was a rude and unlikeable nineteen year old who needed thirty lashes. Then we would see if his blood was royal.

There was not a faction in the land who could tolerate him outside of drunks, homosexuals, prostitutes and his blind parents. Now it seems he has the French disease, but still he could linger for fifty years. How fortunate he is having a bad spell. Sending him to Kirk o' Fields furnished the perfect solution. Soon he and his queer valet will be blown to smithereens. He always loved fireworks and was fascinated with weapons. This will be a fitting end. How she ever loved him, even briefly, was hard to comprehend. Compared to Bothwell he seemed a woman. She was more masculine when dressed in men's garb.

Once they killed him they realized the lords may pursue them. They had a plan that would force their marriage. Bothwell would kidnap her to protect her and then rape her. No one would stop the ceremony. She smiled and you could see white snowflakes were her teeth. As usual she would be doing the raping. He would lie beneath her whilst she wiggled above. They would make love and sink into the cushion of pleasure. What a cooperative prisoner she would be. Yes, tonight the gunpowder would be the salve to ease the pain of Darnley. Bothwell was just what Scotland needed. He had been fiercely loyal to her and hers. Not once had he taken a bribe, rather would he live in penury. The fact that he was not a fanatical Protestant was the icing on the wedding cake. He would help find the middle path that had been covered and grown over with weeds, mangled bushes and John Knox.

Mary's eyes alighted across the room. They scanned the table and appreciated the finely made venison. It had been marinated in wild garlic and herbs. The bread was hot and steam still rose out of the bowl to announce its arrival. Roots of every variety including her favorite parsnip looked fresh and healthy. Kirk o' Fields was masquerading as a sumptuous castle tonight in order to please the king. He was not well and Mary knew festivity would be the best diversion. His life was a diversion; he contributed nothing but wastefulness and greed to the planet. Soon he would be out of her sight blown to the underworld where he could rule forever. No longer would she have to look across the table as he ate with his mouth opened. What she once thought was a sensual lower lip she saw weighed down with overconsumption. Once she nibbled on that mouth like it was an apple, but the worms had come out in droves and exposed his inner ugliness. If she did not murder him his disease would rot him from the inside. He deserved a slow painful death, but she could not afford the time. How she loathed him. Although she did not love Francis and the marriage had never been consummated because of his delicate manly deficiency, she cared for him deeply. Had he not been king it would not have mattered. Always he would have been good and kind. He must be in heaven appalled at the latest marriage.

He had failed in his duty to protect her from the lords. All of Europe fed her to the wolves of the highlands without a thought of her suffering. She had been advised by a wise Frenchman to remain in France and enjoy her dowager position. She would enjoy a lifetime income and live out her life in luxury. France had opened her arms and embraced the porcelain queen doll, a gift from their Scottish ally. Together they formed an alliance against England, so strong; the entire world feared their combined forces could bring England down. France and Scotland were tired of England's endless shenanigans. It never stopped, the Hundred Year War, the Rough Wooing, the constant building up of arms and navy by Henry and now Elizabeth. This marriage was a symbol of their unity in beliefs, politics and spirit. History might have taken Mary to such different ends. It is unstoppable the direction that time paves along the way of life. Abruptly a great mountain rose and Mary was stopped in her path. Looking back she can still see Cali in the mist as she waves goodbye to her French maids. She hugs her terrier close for she will never leave him behind. Her friends stood on the shore and were soon shrouded in the morning mist. Once they were enveloped and gone forever, she had a foreboding feeling that pulled her heart like a loose anchor to the bottom of the darkest sea. Although she had never been seasick, she felt weak and quickly retired to her cabin where instead of dreams she encountered nightmares. She was riding her horse through a pleasant meadow where the heather was blooming, throwing the sunlight back to the sky. It was not the Mary of today, but a much younger princess version. She seemed fragile as glass, but her steed thought her made of leather and jagged rocks. Suddenly, the sky became as black as a crow. Behind her she could hear and feel the galloping of a horse in hot pursuit. When she turned in mortal fear there was Henry VIII carrying his son Edward. But the Prince of Wales was dead in his lap, pale and limp. But the stubborn king would not accept this. Instead he screamed that Mary would marry his son or every man, woman and child in Scotland would feel his rough and vulgar wrath. With this she woke sweaty and restless as the merciless ocean that carried her vessel towards certain doom.

Chapter 7

Mary hurried back across Edinburgh borders late that February night. There was no moon and this had been planned. Defying nature, some celestial light had traveled from eons away to give sparkle to the icy twisted naked tree limbs that bowed to her. She rode astride toward Holyrood house. There was not a woman of privilege who would give up the ease of the side saddle. Yet, Mary felt the freedom of a king as she spread her legs for the entire world to see. It was to her advantage. She held a closer affinity to her beast and rode faster. It gave her dexterity and she felt secure in the saddle. The thrill of the ride was inexplicable. She relished the tempest wind that romanced her face. Private places gave her surprising little pleasures. She had been riding too hard and she and the animal were winded. Instinctively she pulled back the reigns. The pace was slower now as were her thoughts. Her heart was still pounding. The die was cast and nothing would stop Bothwell and his henchmen. Her servant had followed her orders to the letter. In a dither he arrived late in the evening, breathless he informed the queen she must hasten to Holyrood. There was an urgent state matter that required her immediate attention. Darnley was already in a drunken stupor. He could not thank his darling queen enough for her gifts of various ales. He seemed almost grateful for her company and announced he was feeling much cured.

She could almost smell the gunpowder. It was like a sweet perfume. If only Bothwell would have allowed her to light the fuse. It would have been the most defining moment of her life. And for certain, it would be the most pleasurable. Had she been male he would have invited her to the task. Fortunately, what she lacked in brawn was made up in unsurpassed beauty and a magnetic personality that brought men to their knees. Not even women could hide the alarm of jealousy when she entered a room with her favorite pup.

There were so many who wished Darnley dead. Homer's Cyclops was much more popular. No one would dare accuse her of such a deed. It was her sovereign right to kill a defective child king over whom she ruled. There was not a book with enough parchment to list all of his enemies. It would take local sheriffs and Privy Council a century to solve this convoluted murder. This would blow up the past and make room for a sensible man to run this desolate nation that longed to be tamed. Bothwell was her man and always had been. She remembered when she was a young girl and Bothwell had attended the French court. She was intrigued. Their eyes met and she could feel his strength. She was proud that a Scotsman was so handsome. Across time and the English Channel they have been reunited by romantic love and the death bond they signed in blood.

Soon all of her troubles would be put to rest. Darnley was really having a fun- filled evening; meanwhile the gunpowder was being poured in the dungeon directly under his bed. He seemed totally unaware of the revolting postulates that were bursting out like the eruption of tiny volcanoes. Soon his ravaged face would be forced to wear a mask like Cesare Borgia. He managed to survive to the ripe old age of sixty four, dying by the sword as he lived. However, the French disease had claimed him early in life spoiling his good looks. Luckily, Darnley had shown little interest in the marital bed since the conception of James VI. This is when he started his carousing in earnest. Literally just after leaving his son's baptism the sickness gripped him like the plague.

What a coward he had proved at the baptism. Why had he not fled to France or Spain as he had threatened when she refused him the crown matrimonial? Why, she would rather bestow it upon her hawk, Hinkley, who was brave and regal in his bearing. With one swoop he would peck out her enemy's eyes, while Darnley would desert a battle of toy soldiers. Why had he bothered attending? He remained in his private chamber fearful of the lord's wrath. He had tainted her love for Sterling Castle that day. How thankful she had been to depart Christmas day for Drummond Castle, where she would spend the holidays away from his vileness. That was her favorite yuletide gift.

A group of puppeteers entered the room which brought her mind back to the scene. How she loved puppet shows and had spent her childhood directing many. Now, Darnley was smiling at her waving his snot filled hanky. He kissed his hand and blew it toward her. Playing the good wife and decoy she accepted the gesture. She sent his fool to refill his goblets for always he had two or three in front of him. He was the poster child for the seven deadly sins, gluttony being his favorite and avarice not far behind. He was shoving sweetmeats into his mouth like it was his last meal. However did he know? Oblivious to his fate, you could hear his foul laughter and singing that sounded like a croaking frog.

Soon he would fall into the black abyss of death and all of Scotland would rejoice. As soon as her courier whispered that she was needed at Holyrood regarding an urgent state matter, she took her leave. By then her husband was so drunk his face was plastered on the table drooling on his favorite tablecloth. What a relief it was to head back into the night where she could escape him and the foul breath of his disease that mercury had failed to cure.

Chapter 8

Mary Livingston, one of the four favored Marys, was an earthly beauty. The prettiest by far of the queen's ladies in attendance, her blond hair was abundant, a great asset in obtaining the attention of the wealthiest men in the kingdom. Her eyes, as blue as an ultramarine sky, missed very little enjoying the attention. Although she was a seasoned spy, she retained likeable qualities and was kind to a fault. Fragile and the height of femininity, courtiers wished to take her in their arms and care for her. When she walked with her majesty in the garden they became the bloom. Educated and well bred, her companionship was treasured. She was as perceptive as a sorceress and it benefited the queen to take her advice.

Today she was obviously not herself. She sat in stunned silence. Tears poured out of eyes where fear also was apparent. The deed was done and the streets of Edinburg ran with Darnley's blood. The queen's subjects were outraged and sought justice for Prince James VI. They wanted him avenged and the murderers drawn and quartered. This was an unforeseen outcome. Not one person in the inner sanctum expected pity from the people. The lords were taking advantage and acting outraged when all knew of their extensive hatred for the ineffectual king. They had been biding their time, she was fully aware of the Craigmiller bond that the Earl of

Moray and many lords had signed months ago. It was Darnley's death warrant and they were planning his demise. Now they were acting as if this was the worst possible scenario. Her most faithful and skilled servant worked at Craigmiller Castle and had informed her of the plot. She begged Mary and Bothwell to wait for others to take the risk, but to no avail. They were far too deep in romantic heat and anxious for Bothwell to rule alongside of his love. Now the lords would conquer the couple, hanging them with their own rope.

Mary had gone into mourning and would remain in seclusion in Holyrood for forty days, as was the custom. This was a blessing and would help calm the storm. She had dressed the queen in her widow weeds and no one would gaze upon her. She failed to tell Mary that one of Cecil's minions was at this moment sketching the crime scene. Darnley's body had been returned to the palace and was now being embalmed. The people were crying for an open coffin wishing to view the body. Mary had already been informed by her spies at Kirk o' field that he was found in one piece, with his valet, dead in the garden strangled to death.

When Mary informed the queen, she was in shock. She refused to believe the blast did not do its job. Although it had shook Edinburgh to the core he remains intact, but thankfully dead. How the lords must be gloating. They would have savored taking that neck of Darnley's and breaking it off his head.

Hundreds stood in line casting lots to see who would have the pleasure of exterminating the rat. They will soon rob the queen of her throne; she could feel it in her bones. They have manipulated and gone underground to plot against the Crown and yet they will win. The queen is pure, untouched, she must rule. This nonsense will lead to a bitter end. It is the ultimate feud and only one faction will be left standing on Scottish soil.

Who had informed Darnley? They had been so clandestine. He was naked carrying his nightshirt, as if alerted and gone in haste. Perhaps Bothwell's men had been clumsy and the noise woke his valet, for surely Darnley was in a drunken slumber.

Holyrood was damp and uncomfortable. The fire danced and flares licked the stones in the grate until they were black. It did its best to warm the beautiful women that faithfully added logs and vigorously pumped the bellows. How sad and frightened she looked, not at all her delightful self.

Why had the queen not listened to her advice and left Bothwell to his homely wife Jean Gordon? She knows he was seeking an annulment so he would be free to marry Her Majesty. She had a terrible premonition that the lords would despise this more than they had the killing of Lord Darnley. Bothwell was their greatest nemesis. He had been loyal to Marie Guise and Mary. They could not bribe him into treachery. He was not an extremist in his Protestant faith. He despised John Knox. The list was endless and went back decades. They would act out their vendetta soon. The road to destruction was wide. John Knox was right about that. Those two were hurrying down that lane at this very moment and will not look back. Beware of the precipices ahead and the fall from grace that waits.

How fortunate she was that soon she would marry, escaping this tumultuous time. She had led a privileged life. Always close to the queen, she was like a sister. What folly had befallen her once charmed life? Lord Maitland would make a brilliant husband. He was a respected politician and had been Secretary of State. Although he could be devious she was certain she could persuade him to behave. He was quite enamored with her and loved the feel of her upper hand.

Outside the cold would not relent. She could hear goblins moaning and the ancients chanting. The old kings ruthless and long dead were turning in their graves. The order of the monarchy would soon falter and a hundred years of scheming and plotting would end and the lords would finally prevail, of this she was certain. Closing her eyes she hoped to escape the pain and fell into a welcome sleep that she wished she could share with the queen, who could not rest.

Chapter 9

Bothwell held the damming placard in his hand, reading it in disbelief. Everyone in Edinburg was accusing Mary and himself of the crime. Elizabeth and Catherine De Medici wrote letters to Mary urging her to find the king's killer with haste and have an expedient trial. They begged her to think of her honor. Catherine De Medici was her French mother in law and dowager queen of France; they had never had a good relationship when she was married to Francis. Now this was evident to the world. She sent no envoys with sorrowful missives to Scotland regarding the king's death. Gossip was spreading across Europe like the bubonic plague. Bothwell asked Mary not to start a witch hunt; arresting people to throw off the scent would be unjust. Time would heal the wound. He would help her rule in Darnley's place. Soon they would wed and all would be well in the kingdom. Not five minutes after tearing down the filthy poster accusing them of the crime he announced to all of Edinburg the perpetrator would bathe in blood. So many wanted Darnley removed from the realm, yet there was this unexpected backlash. The lords had tried Bothwell for the murder, acquitting him when the evidence was lacking. Still, the placards continued to appear on church doors, inns, the tollbooth and crossroads. The smear continued with great momentum. Bothwell was convinced the lords were behind this campaign. Public opinion against him and his love were on the rise. He was constantly reassuring Mary, yet he was secretly having doubts. The pressure of the lords was overwhelming. He could feel his adrenalin flow at an alarming rate. The contraction in his manhood made his knees buckles. He had few moments of weakness in his life and realized now was the time to seize the moment. Soon he would spirit her off to Dunbar Castle where their plan would come to fruition. Now he was certain the lords had set all of this up. They were working in earnest to turn the people against Mary. This way they could easily force Mary to abdicate.

He must act as swiftly as the French swordsman that clipped off Ann Boleyn's head. They must go forward with the kidnap, rape and finally a lawful union. Intertwined, their vines would grow and span across the castle walls. It would be wholesome for her subjects to witness compromise on these ghastly religious matters. He did not believe in God. What nonsense. Never could he reveal this to a soul, not even the queen. When we die it's like the endless expanse of nothingness prior to birth. We cease being once again; free to escape the pains of this earth.

Fortunately, he had secured a bond with the signature of many supporters. It was official approval that he would continue to assist the queen with her rule. Hopefully this would overcome the negative outcry that was foiling their sensible hopes for Scotland.

How he looked forward to spring. Although relatively young he could feel arthritis creeping into his youthful bones. He took the pamphlet out of his doublet and threw it into the river that had recently started to thaw. If he discovered the author he would soon feel the current that would drag him out to sea.

Chapter 10

The Earl of Moray removed the Craigmiller bond from his doublet. It bore his signature as well as the lords with the greatest clout. This was an agreement that they would plot to kill the king. It was drawn up for the good of the kingdom, a powerful device. Had Bothwell and his sister an ounce of patience they would have been outside of this matter. But now the onus was on them.

How they had all voted against Darnley from the onset. He had such nerve questioning Moray's very own holdings, informing the queen she was too generous with her brother. He was just another Catholic who wished to upset the apple cart. He had the leadership qualities of a skunk and at the end his disease made him smell like one, quite repulsive. All of the lords were overjoyed when Mary quickly lost interest in him. He was a transparent fool with superficial good looks and Lennox trappings. They zealously signed her bond issuing them to render obedience to the queen alone. That had been sufficient at the time.

But the death sentence that the lords would employ upon Darnley came after the Rizzo murder conspiracy. Following an investigation the queen exiled all but her foul husband. He denied any involvement and she was too weak to accept the truth. He was as anxious for the kill as a hunter who has flexed his bow aimed upon a prize buck. She refused to condemn royal blood. It would be a sacrilege. As he expected she missed his attention and sensible guidance. It did not take her long to welcome her brother back with open arms. He could really love her if she was not such an idiot. A replica of her mother she repeated mistakes and continued to irk the best of men. Her beauty caused him no pain. He would rather she be stone ugly with a level head. Parliament was lost without him as well. Once she capitulated it was in earnest. She restored all of his holdings and more making him the richest man in Scotland. Although the wealth was comforting his greatest desire was to implement power. It benefited Scotland. He was a patriotic man and truly valued his country.

The embers were cold and the servant would not relight it until the morning. His wealth did not stop him from being parsimonious. Firewood was a precious commodity. The winter was ending and he had further rationed its use. With great care he took the parchment on which the bond was etched and placed an edge over the candle's flame. Quietly he watched it curl and obliterate the proof of the lords' intentions to murder Darnley.

The air around Craigmiller Castle would not settle. The wind forced the trees to bend to its will. Branches shook and some were torn away by the force of winter taking its leave. It would not give into the coming season without a fight. The lords were the wind and Mary was the tree that soon would bow to their command, abdicating in favor of her son, James VI. He would then rule as regent to his nephew bringing back the order the monarchs had carelessly let slip away.

Chapter 11

As the word regicide was whispered a
thousand times through the land Mary tried to
continue to rule. She signed documents ratifying the
Acts of the Reformation Parliament of 1560. She
had previously refused to do so but now she needed
Parliament's cooperation if she was to marry
Bothwell. She was shocked that lands and
restitution had been provided to men implicated in
Darnley's murder. At the moment it seemed
Bothwell was in control and no one was blocking
their unofficial joint rule. He was acquitted of
Darnley's murder and that was heaven-sent.
Bothwell was so confident he gave the lords a
sumptuous dinner at his favorite tavern, The Lion's
Head, in Edinburgh. When all had their fill
Bothwell produced yet another bond that read they
would support him against his enemies. Mary was
surprised that both Catholic and Protestant lords had
signed it. She did not feel at ease as she read it. She
feared this was all more smoke and mirrors and the
lords were secretly rallying against the couple. She
had been so ill since the incident. Taking refuge at
Seton had helped but she was glad to be back in
Edinburgh. Soon she would visit her son at Sterling
and their plan would finally unfold. Only a chosen
few realized that they planned to wed and she felt a
stabbing pain for she was certain there may be
objections that would be difficult to overcome. That
is why Bothwell would have to pretend to force

himself on her at Dunbar Castle. To salvage her honor all would agree to the marriage. Mary knew her brother would be against their union. This would be difficult, but somehow they would prevail.

Chapter 12

Sterling Castle brought back fond memories that made her sad at the same time. She remembered her beloved pony, Princess. She had been terribly sad to leave her when Marie of Guise sent her off to France. She was just a little girl, but already wise to the privileges and ways of royalty. When her father died he had named her cousin James Hamilton, Earl of Arran, the second person of the realm. He was also second in line to the throne at that time. He was Protestant and there was much contention between him and her Catholic mother. He signed a treaty at Greenwich enforcing her to be delivered to Henry the VIII court when she was ten in order to be groomed to marry his son Edward. This is when destiny took a sharp turn, she was spirited off to France, promised to the Dauphine. She would grow up in the luxury of the royal chateaux, Chambord and Fontainebleau as Henry invaded Scotland when the treaty was broken.

This castle was always a busy place, especially in the spring. All of the floor reeds were changed and the place started to smell fresh and clean. The little prince was fawned over day and night. He was pampered by Protestant aristocrats handpicked by the lords to ensure his safety, education and well- being. She wondered what he thought as people bowed and curtseyed to him all day. For now they were alone. She had sent everyone away, longing to share a peaceful time with her son. She forgot that today when she left with her small retinue, Bothwell would be waiting. For a moment she thought of calling off the escapade. Mayhap she will forego her relationship with Bothwell in exchange for a quiet life with her child. She picked him up and sang a lullaby her mother had taught her as a child. She laid him in his royal bassinet as he quickly fell into the easy sleep of a babe. He wore a little smile and made sweet breathy sounds that made it even more difficult for her to depart. She stood above him for a very long time and wept as if she may never see him again.

Chapter 13

They met as planned at the bridge that spanned the Almond River. Tree limbs reached out still ice covered from an unseasonably cold night. Their buds were insisting on an audience with the queen but Lord Frost continued to usurp the season. Bothwell had a large force of men all with weapons brandished. She feigned surprise and allowed them to lead her towards Dunbar Castle with little resistance. He informed the party loud and clear, that he was taking the queen to safety for there was an insurrection planned in Edinburgh upon her return. Inside she started to panic and harbored second thoughts. Outside she appeared calm and in control but it was a weak façade. However, once Bothwell rode to her side, his magnetism was overwhelming and she gave little resistance. She could feel her love for him swell inside. All of her female parts tingled and she immediately entertained lusty thoughts. There was no resisting him. He kissed her hand before they marched and gazed knowingly into her eyes. It was hypnotic and calming giving her strength to a final commitment regardless of the outcome. At that moment they signed the most important bond of their lives.

Chapter 14

The old Celtic gods still commanded their underworld, conjuring up constellations that were portents for mortal men. Their ancient chants would decide the fate of queens. The icy rain was like a barrage of tiny arrows but Dunbar Castle withstood the pummeling like it was deflecting another attack of the Rough Wooing. The castle worked like camouflage. Its walls of boulders seemed like any other hunk of rocky cliffs. It appeared to have built itself, like a natural wonder. It was the perfect hideout to regroup like bandits instead of royalty.

They were relieved when they rode towards their destination. It was a welcome sight, for all were weary and desperate for rest except for Bothwell. He was as hard as the stone that laid its foundation. He was only happy that it would be a refuge for their love and lust. All of the worries and gyrations of the past months had provided a dearth of sexual activity. There had been little energy or opportunity for their favorite pastime.

They wasted no time once they pulled up the drawbridge. Mary asked her servants to go enjoy some bread and wine as they escaped into the inner sanctum of the castle. He slowly removed her wet cloak and peeled off her damp garments. They would soon be wed and rule Scotland. The thought was giving him an erection that would last the night.

The lords and subjects would accept their union or they must face civil war.

The waves pounded like madmen. The ice had a pact with winter and was fending off the spring. Mean and aggressive it reminded him of how he must behave if he did not get the cooperation they were demanding. Darnley was dead. Their goal was so complete his corpulent body was now dancing in hell like a ghoulish marionette. There was not a pit deep enough to rid the earth of that royal fop. He had inherited all of the bad traits from the Yorks and the Lancasters. They were a confused dynasty of rulers. You were beautiful and brilliant, able to lead a country with a cool head and iron fist. Or you were born a complete fool, like Darnley. Who did not want him dead? Only his Lennox parents who spoiled him into oblivion. Always they filled his head with the folly of succession, a certain path to the gallows or at best life in the tower. A shady and uncomfortable end where one could only hope to be rescued by insanity, as was Henry the VI. William Cecil's spies were well informed of his plot with France, and Spain to join with Irish rebels. Darnley had the audacity to believe they would oust Elizabeth and place him on the throne. What rubbish. He forced himself to forget these aggravating thoughts and concentrate on his true love. His sole errand was to please his soon- to -be wife, which would be the easiest task of all.

In the morning she lay naked next to her amour. She whispered that she felt they had conceived a child that would be second in line to James VI. They rejoiced in this possibility, welcoming more heirs. He looked lovingly upon her youthful limbs. Her stomach was taut and belied a woman who had given birth to any child. He marveled that underneath, her womb was like a treasure, more precious than the royal jewels. He ran his fingers over her small plump breasts. They matched her entirety. If he was an artist he would choose to chisel rather than paint her upon canvas. She had too many angles and small muscles that surprised a man as he rubbed his hand below her neck. A tightly curved buttock was always his hands' final resting place as she looked down upon him with complete compliance.

They laughed together when they realized the news of Mary's abduction would soon be known to all in Scotland and England. Spies were as common as the spider. Bothwell was glad that the world would have knowledge of his intentions, for there was no going back to his homely wife Jean Gordon or the simple life of a lord. Mary yawned and stretched like a seductive incubus and they soon fell back into the ancient rhythm of love.

Chapter 15

Early in May as Queen Elizabeth was promising Lady Lennox revenge for her son's death, Bothwell led Mary back into the gates of Edinburgh. May bloomed as victorious as them. Its splendor adorned Scotland like the flower Mary wore in her hair for Bothwell's pleasure. He led her by the horse's bridle like he owned her. They entered Edinburgh Castle where a great many men would guard her, ensuring no one would have an interview with the queen. That week Bothwell obtained his annulment. He informed Mary they could now move forward. She was free to move to her comfortable home at Holyrood.

Meanwhile, the entire capital was in an uproar when they announced they would marry. This seemed to enrage more than Darnley's murder. Despite the attitude of the nation the marriage contract was signed. There was not a person who could believe Mary would wed a man who had raped and humiliated her. It seemed obvious they had conspired to kill Darnley so they could rule. They had set their own trap.

Everyone was outraged and not at all backing the nuptial bands. The lords made it clear that they were against the marriage and a current of tension rose across the capitals that even the most innocent and uninformed citizen could not ignore.

Bothwell looked upon his bride with great pleasure. Although she was still wearing her widow weeds her beauty could not be denied.

Chapter 16

Mary could not believe how quickly events turned against them. Marrying Bothwell had been her downfall; not the killing of Darnley. That was just an excuse to turn the world against them. The lords did an excellent job at making even the Catholics hate her. They felt she was a heretic and bigamist. She could not believe what was happening. She could not rise from her bed. Bothwell was unable to console her as she lay in bed with her terrier day and night. Even her confessor ran back to France horrified at her behavior. She could feel civil war brewing in her bones. Her closest informants had advised her that all of the lords had left Edinburgh and were planning on marching against Bothwell. They wanted to capture and kill him for forcing Mary to marry him. They would prefer Satan to rule their country. The lords were at Sterling working to protect the prince and attempting to raise an army of four thousand men. This was the rebellion brewing. Mary had feared they would take this action all along. She shook under her silk sheets and feared her future. Now he comes with the worst possible news. When Bothwell had gone to Edinburgh Castle to ensure they could enter this safe haven he discovered he had been betrayed by his best man. Baxter, the man who had lit the fuse at Kirk o' Field would not allow him to enter. He must have been fearful that if Bothwell was caught he would be implicated in the murder. He had ultimately agreed to turn over this decisive castle to the rebel lords. This was a mighty blow for without this fortress they would have to devise a new strategy.

Mary finally realized that she must rise to the occasion. She was an anointed queen above the lords and would conquer them once and for all. They would regret their hundred years of subterfuge and plots to undermine the monarchy. She had all of her plates and even a gold christening font melted down to raise revenue for the troops that remained loyal to her cause.

Chapter 17

Under the cover of darkness the couple and their loyal followers left Hoyrood for Borthwick Castle.

Bothwell had left Mary to muster up more troops. She remained at Borthwick Castle and had never felt so alone in her life. Now she must flee. The lords had come demanding Bothwell's surrender after calling him filthy names and firing numerous rounds of weapons. When she appeared at the wall they begged her to depart with them. After patiently waiting for the queen to join them they finally retreated to Edinburgh Castle. They could no longer deny Mary's culpability in the nefarious plot.

It was a warm June night, lit only by fireflies and a crescent moon, dark enough for Mary to escape Borthwick. Black clouds were veiling the stars whose ominous prediction could not be altered. Jupiter was rising and Pegasus was in the perfect quadrant that gave birth to disaster and defeat of sovereigns. The lords would soon return with a vengeance to find her gone. She shimmied down a rope dressed as a man with the dexterity of an acrobat. She hastened to mount her horse and with several of Bothwell's faithful servants she galloped off to meet up with her lover at Black Castle. The medieval tower rose out of the night like a demon. It did not look a place she would like to go in the best of times. It was unbelievable that the treasonous lords were planning to cut off the head of their rightful queen. Without a true queen there would be no justice for the people. Her majesty's subjects would be forced to drink the bitter dredges the lords would discard with no regard for the common man. For them she would fight to the death. When she arrived a scout informed her that she was to hasten to Dunbar Castle where Bothwell had gathered a significant force that would march against the lords. In the morning they would attack Edinburgh and regain her kingdom. He swore allegiance to the Crown and knelt before the goddess of a queen whose beauty could stun most men into instant obedience.

They spent their last night linked together like two minks. He had found the strength to please her. She had changed into her armor at Black Castle. When he saw her she seemed a modern day Joan of Arc. Her bravery and beauty blinded him and his followers. When dressed as a man she seemed androgynous and somehow this aroused his manhood. She was a creature the Druid priests had conjured up in their mystical forest thousands of years ago. She was delivered to Marie of Guise by the raven warrior Goddess Morrigan. Her long legs held him like a vise. Not once did she cry or weaken in her resolve to join forces with him. Her weakness had passed and was left behind at Holyrood. He adored her; she was both a warrior goddess and Venus. If the lords had the pleasure of seeing her naked, they would pledge their lives to her, drop their swords and grovel at her feet.

Chapter 18

By now the summer was warming up the bones of Scotsmen after a brutal winter. Most were content to watch over their flock of sheep or tend to their precious crops. They could not be aware that the fault line was trembling and would soon slip, changing the geography of their leadership inexorably.

It was to the day, after one month of marriage the newlyweds are defeated at Carberry Hill. Not a shot is fired. Yet, everything had gone as planned. They met at the predestinated location, she with a small force and cannon. Bothwell had gathered close to two thousand men. In the middle of the night he had gone to call in favors, so they would have as many allies as possible. He was confident most signers would honor the bond promising allegiance to Bothwell and the queen. Unfortunately, many men started deserting as soon as Bothwell left. When they met close to Carberry Hill she realized immediately they were outnumbered and refused to have useless bloodshed. The lords were four thousand strong and as she looked up at their mound of armor her hand trembled on her reins. She laid a flag over them so ashamed was she of her condition. Heralds were sent back and forth across the lines as the lords continued to hold a banner crying for justice for Prince James VI. The parleying went on for several hours until Mary agreed to surrender if they allowed Bothwell and his men to retreat. She was hoping Lord Huntley or the Hamiltons would send reinforcement. They had always been great allies and friends of the Crown. But as the shadows grew longer she faced that all was lost for now. Mary shivered as she thought of how Bothwell had begged her to retreat to Dunbar at his side, but Mary refused. The lords were content to let Bothwell flee now, Mary was the prize. He was so privy to all of their plots to kill Darnley and disrupt the queen it would be best if he would vanish. This would end the marriage as well, a tidy solution. The queen would soon be in an impenetrable prison where she would be tried for regicide and forced to abdicate.

Mary rode her horse slowly next to the lord who had tied her horse to his. She did not recognize him under his chain of a helmet. He seemed to purposely cover his face and refused to converse. Somehow she surmised it was Lord Boyd of the Privy Council. It was the way he was sitting so erect and proudly showing off his elitist qualities. Then she noticed his family crest ring as he grabbed the reins tighter. She would remember this and seek her revenge.

Mary was glad she had given herself up so Bothwell may escape. He was their best chance to round up a league of soldiers that would crush the lords in one final blow. June had never felt so hot.

The horses and men smelled like nothing at the French Court. The sun baked down on her like a punishing god. There were not three merging suns as had been at the Battle of Mortimer Cross spelling a Yorkish victory for King Edward IV against his Lancastrian foe. It was just one searing ball that was not her friend. It was, in fact, the face of defeat. She heard someone whisper, under the braying of the horses, they were taking her to Lochleven Castle. If they realized how intimately she knew every window and crevice of that destination they would soon change direction. Also, it would be an ideal location to give birth to Bothwell's coming heir if she could not escape. However, she felt that after extended parleying they would realize she was a truly anointed queen and quickly release her. God gave her wisdom that she passed down to the mere mortals beneath her. She remains somewhere between heaven and earth. That is exactly where she would remain. Bothwell would soon see to that.

She still felt the final kiss that Bothwell had so passionately burned onto her willing lips. With great audacity he sent his tongue inside of her mouth without a care for propriety. His impudence was most welcome and she would not release from his embrace until he finally sped away kicking up dust and stones. How shocked those prissy lords must have been at such a sight. Now they have witnessed the love flow between them and hopefully accept her resolve for them to rule as one.

As they approached the castle she began to have doubts for the citizens cried out against her and with great disrespect threw bread and awful things at her person. This had been, so far, the worst day of her life.

Chapter 19

Morton the most powerful of the lords, second only to the Earl of Moray looked into space with the eyes of a snake. He remembered the lords as they sat with their long beards and pointy noses. All cheeks were burned red from the winter that was as adamant as her majesty hell-bent on causing discomfort. Yet the rivers were thawing unlike their resolve to force Mary to abdicate or worst. The die was cast; leave it to those Englishmen to state events so precisely. They do not dally around with words or invasions. You do not encounter them arguing a fig over which religion is the guiding force of their nation. William Cecil is a devout Protestant and Queen Elizabeth follows his sound advice. She is fortunate to have such an astute secretary and advisor. He has laid a spy ring so deftly throughout the known world he will know when Phillip II moves his bowels.

England had the good sense to tear down the monasteries and decorate their Tudor walls and tables with silver plates and goblets from their unholy altar. And when a Catholic queen reared her ugly head as Mary I, the Lord quickly cut her down. Now a level- headed bonny redheaded jewel of a girl rules England with great authority. Scotland must soon join with England and will when James VI ascends the throne. Cecil's spies had informed him that Elizabeth's first reaction had been to punish the Scottish lords. This was fortunate for Mary, for if the lords felt England was with them they would have immediately killed their queen, with impunity. However, Cecil finally convinced her it would best suit England to side with the Protestant lords. Even the Pope had given up on Mary despising her now as much as Elizabeth for her blasphemous ways.

How relieved he was that they had conquered their errant queen. What a tribulation these past six months had been. The lord had arrested and tortured over sixty suspects and formally charged Mary and Bothwell with Darnley's murder. Certain "Casket Letters" which also surfaced written to Bothwell in Mary's own hand and signed by the queen have sealed her fate. Although he suspected they were forged he would never admit his belief. Whatever trickery it took to bring down this queen so be it. They had these letters in their possession and they would be used as evidence in the coming trial. Now she is sitting on pins and needles in Lochleven Castle, as she deserves. Let her feel the pain and think long and hard upon her transgressions. First her mother interfered. That whore of Babylon has given birth to a Jezebel. John Knox is quite right calling her that name in his speeches. She never ruled with sense, listening to that Italian fool David Rizzo. Why not heed the advice of the lords, whose word she should savor. They begged her not to marry Darnley.

Queen Elizabeth had thrown Lady Lennox, his interfering mother, into the tower for crafting the marriage that would put their house closer to the English throne. Mary may as well have wed Lucifer. Her beauty has confounded her. Though she be a gifted sportswoman and deft at bookish things, her sense was bought from an Edinburgh prostitute. Why did she bother to kill Darnley? Others would have chewed him up and spit him into the Firth of Forth. The Earl of Moray is now in his glory knowing his half sister has performed his dirty work. He did not so much as lift a finger. He is everywhere and nowhere. His luck runs like a river stocked with golden carp abundant. He conspires to kill David Rizzo with Darnley. Then Mary exiles the Earl to England and proclaims her husband innocent, though he is the driving force as guilty as Moray. When pardoned and returned he must look outwardly upon Darnley with no remorse. Meanwhile, his hatred bubbles like Vesuvius. His greatest wish has now come true. He will be regent of Scotland, guardian to his nephew, James VI. It sounded too much like a Shakespearean play to be real and true. But Mary will soon be tried for plotting to kill the king and possibly jailed for life much like Henry VI was held in the Tower while Edward IV usurped his throne.

The lords would now be free to impress Protestantism on the masses who must obey. John Knox would have free rein to preach and be followed to the letter. James VI would never know his Catholic mother or have ears for any papal nonsense. Someday, if Elizabeth does not soon drop a viable successor from her loins, James VI will rule this island whole.

His turnip soup was getting cold. Losing interest he pushed it aside and pulled out the parchment from inside his cape. He read the indictment over several times and glanced at the signatures of every lord. It was an authentic and powerful instrument of the law. The Privy Council will act upon it with no remorse. They were now turning the pages of history, not the queen of hearts. She belonged in a deck of cards where no harm could come to her. She was only good for lovemaking and providing an heir. He rolled up the final draft with great precision placing the ancient seal upon it like a deadly kiss. He blew out the candle and sat in the dark for a long time, satisfied that the lords had won.

Chapter 20

All was lost, almost. Luckily, Bothwell had escaped and would soon afford a rescue. He had great powers all along the border, as well as the continent. Not once did he take a bribe from England or any foreign state. Mary had bestowed several earned titles and fortunes upon him during her reign. How unfortunate he could not free her at this very moment. What a horror to be a prisoner at Lochleven Castle under the lords' lock and key. She still clung earnestly to the belief that they would negotiate with a truly anointed queen who should be ruling England, as well. All knew Elizabeth was a bastard. Mary could bring balance back to Britannia. The scales made even. The mass would be said with no trepidation. Protestants could worship in their empty halls, she had no care. Her religion would, of course, always be the true one, as she was the true Queen of Scotland, France and England. Her strength should be abundant, her power endless. Her reign unpunished. To her advantage there was a faction of subjects remaining loyal to her command. At this moment they were hatching a plan to free their beloved sovereign. She had read the cryptic messages with joy.

Mary looked down at her long tapered fingers, frustrated friends that were entwined together. Pacing back and forth in her lavish prison, she waited for a signal that would release her from the lords and their nasty contrivances. Perhaps her mother had made a grave error in forbidding her marriage to Edward. Instantly she would have been awarded the crown matrimonial, in splendor. Henry VIII may have been a wise man who knew how to line up a succession to the throne. He had every one of his whims burned into the book of his law, upon death. Edward and Mary, it did have a nice ring. How different her destiny would have never known France or Bothwell. Life would be filled with constraints. Surely she would be a sexual midget. David Rizzo never would have led her on the path to intellectual and political understanding. How she had loved playing cards and instruments with him late into the starry night that hung above like their private audience. Sitting by the roaring fire he passed knowledge onto her like thick oak logs that fueled an endless flame. How she loved his mind, though most found him ugly he was to her as Michelangelo's David. An Italian aristocrat, they met at the French Court and were, hence, inseparable. Traveling to Scotland together, he became her greatest advisor. No one met with her unless he approved. Yet, the errant lords and Darnley had slaughtered him at her dinner table, in her private closet. Now he lays desecrated in a pauper's grave. How he longed to just look upon her breasts. He would kneel before her in wonder of them. His worship encompassed her very being. Their private relationship was taken to the highest level a monarch could afford. Rizzo had always been her man. How she felt the terror as he screamed for her to save him, while she sat helpless and almost full term in her pregnancy. How she had not miscarried is beyond wonder. Over and over they stabbed him until his heart dissolved under the cruel blade of traitors. How quickly she fled to Bothwell fearing her assassination would follow. Jealousy was the deadly sin that murdered David. Only Bothwell could protect her from those who would seek her dead in her own Holyrood. Regicide has become as innocent as a game of croquet to these rebel lords.

Mary closed her eyes for a moment and the wind became David Rizzo's voice. His ghost lingered just outside, wailing softly in the night. There was great peril about, she must escape to France. Their king will send troops against the Earl of Moray, her treacherous half-brother. She should sail directly to Normandy dressed as a man. It was her favorite disguise, loving breaches and doublets. In better times she would walk around Edinburgh in her masculine attire. No would guess her the queen. She would watch her subjects go about their daily routine without caution. The washerwomen would curse the fish monger. The butcher would cut up his pig; like it was Henry VIII, bones cracking and blood flying. Prostitutes would approach her like hucksters attempting to sell their wares in the alleyways, unknowingly, to the Queen of Scotland.

Mayhap the Rough Wooing could have been avoided. There may instead have been a gentle embrace, the two nations united by royal consent. But, her mother was a French Catholic and could never abide by the union. With little thought to the far reaching consequences of her actions and much sorrow, she had Mary set sail. The winds blowing off the coast and the waves slapping caused a loud and thunderous adieu. How she had missed her pony Princess and loving mother's touch. She could feel her guidance and tenderness blow across the channel like a lullaby making her safe and content with her destiny. Innately, she understood her duty as she stood on the bow of the ship like a maidenhead carved and stoic facing the shores of France like a good and brave little princess. Her mother's last kiss still burned her cheek like a hot tear. It had clung there all of these years. But, now it was time to wipe it away and change the channel of time. Soon her allies would emerge to overthrow the evil lords. Scotland would be brought back to its rightful rule. Only Mary Queen of Scots could recognize the needs of her subjects. They would bow to her for she was above all men with only God to answer to.

She was exhausted and bored. Pulling the heavy gilded curtains aside, she found no view. The sun had slipped away like a thief that had robbed the crown jewels. How she longed to saddle up her horse and ride with abandon across the highlands. It was there she would commiserate with the ancient sages. They would lead her to their stone altar and sacrifice the most beautiful virgin in her honor. With a sweep of their hands and nod of their hooded heads, all would be clear. She would consult with her ancestors and drink the brew of wisdom, mixed with the sacrificial blood.

The wind outside would not abate. It howled and licked the icy stone walls without regret. She stood there until her legs could not hold. Finally she surrendered to sleep. The only escape the lost queen could find. For the first time in her life she welcomed the darkness.

Chapter 21

Wicked and wild in its nature, the North Sea tossed Bothwell's sailing vessel, the "Viking," over another rough wave. He clung to the helm like he did to his resolve that he would be victorious. The lords had too many enemies. He would find them and Elizabeth's, as well. So many countries were tired of her abrasive policies, backed by William Cecil. Actually, he was the hatcher of these ideals that made would be allies into armadas. It was hard to concentrate at the helm. But it was just the job for him at the moment, for the task at hand made it his slave. Not for an instant could you rest from the motion of the dark forces below. This is why man loved to sail. He must leave his troubles behind; even the thought of his love could sink a ship, if he inadvertently turned his sails into the wrong path of the wind. Survival is dependent on man tossing overboard all thought not concerning the rudder. Yet, for all of the physical and mental strength that had been bred into his stock over centuries, he could not find the willpower to stop thinking of his queen. Like a lily with her white capped shoulders she stood tall and erect. When he stood beside her he could smell her delicate scent. Her dark eyes were black obsidian and a deadly pool if a man drank from them. Now she was his wife, it was his duty to rescue her, as quickly as a zephyr.

Soon he would have his audience with the King of Denmark, who owed him many a favor. Ships would fly home in a battle to save his love. Other countries would join them. Spain was especially eager to gain control in Britain. Their King Philip II was on a crusade to reinstate the Pope's rule both in England and Scotland. Nothing could keep a good man down, and he was the best on the planet. He had felt his power and abilities as a child sailing his self-made wooden boat on his father's lake. His friends automatically knew he was the leader and always deferred to his desires. He led his childhood friends into many battles, all of which were victorious. Always the favorite, his mother doted on him and his father passed down ancient knowledge that has been invaluable throughout his life. He had always made his family proud and would continue to do so. Lulling him out of his revelry, he heard a mate call from the crow's-nest "land ho!" It was music to his ears.

Chapter 22

After many months of captivity awaiting her trial and judgment Mary finally escaped. She donned her favorite costume dressed as a man. The event was swift and incident free. As time passed and Bothwell failed to reappear with trumpets blaring and horses charging, the guards became lax. A pretty little scullery maid who adored Mary was great help. When Maggie raised her apron over her head the young soldier lost interest in his sworn duty.

The boatswain rowed her and several servants away from Lochleven Castle. He looked at the queen's marble white hands and was amazed that fingers could fascinate him so. Her hands were known throughout the land and revered as a work of art.

Although thankful to be free, Mary could not ignore the pain in her womb. The lost twin boys, Princes that would never have a chance to rule their kingdom, had died inside her. Two male successors, Stuart and Tudor blood ran through their veins that could be traced back to John of Gaunt. What a waste. Now she must flee alone.

How fortunate she was that Bothwell had spies scattered throughout Europe. Servants and visiting envoys supplied cryptic messages that she was genius at interpreting. They were glad to carry her replies and plots abroad with great discretion. How she loved puzzles and games of intrigue growing up in France. Combined with her love of language, mathematics and military skills she was a natural spy.

Her translations were reliable and she had the stealth of a mountain lion. She thought how much being a clever and beautiful queen had always been to her advantage.

She sang quietly to herself as they rowed past the forest whose eyes were a sentinel. Her only subject that would still serve her, watched with deference as they helped cloak her from the enemy. When she sang at court people would gasp at the perfect pitch with an angelic quality. She needed no instrument to accompany her, for she sounded like a bird of paradise. Her interest in music flourished over a lifetime of pursuing her talents and smallest desires. She played the flute as well as the harp and cittern.

Her greatest pleasure was also unexpected. A great diversion, it was a gift from David Rizzo, her murdered advisor. He brought her a puppet show from Italy and she found it would consume her for days. She loved to design the costumes and write dialogue. She would create characters and backdrops of great variety. This was her great love.

Always she would be the voice of the heroine. Her queen puppet would be rescued by a handsome and brave king. A stately horse was built and saddled to carry the two happy royal puppets back to their long lost kingdom.

Her life had been suffocated in sweetness like a sugared plum. Every whim was satisfied. What contrast with her recent life? It was like part two of a Greek play plunging into tragedy. Yet, she could still smell the flowers at Fontainebleau dressed as royalty. She could see herself playing backgammon and cards in the gilded gazebo.

Finally she awoke to her predicament. The lords wanted her abdication. If caught they may imprison her for life. She must run to her cousin Queen Elizabeth for help. She will understand the urgency and reinstate Mary back to her throne. She had been wooed by her surly cousin's father, King Henry VIII. They broke past Hadrian's Wall by the thousands to pursue her. Edward would have his beautiful Princess of Wales if he had to throw all of the children of Scotland into the Firth of Ford. Well, now she was coming of her own free will. It was now her command that the Tudors reach out to her crown. This would be her invasion. She should be ruling England in so many ways and that bastard cousin of hers knows the truth. That is why she has spies everywhere, always fearful of losing her position. This has given birth to the age of total greed and debauchery. No man can have a private thought. Her spies will soon get a word out of everyone to bring to Elizabeth on a silver platter. Well two can play that game. She will help me seek revenge upon the lords for she has seen their hatred for the monarchy and she cannot abide that. It could lead to her undoing. The constant fear of losing her crown will force her to side with royalty, regardless of religious differences. She has realized government's first concern cannot revolve around theology. This is a matter we both have come to accept as wise rulers of our modern time. Clearly she knows the hatred that the lords harbored for Darnley, especially my traitor half brother the Earl of Moray. She will wish to see my standard rise in battle to reclaim my son and throne.

The plan was rolled up on her lap. She would be accompanied by a troop of good men fiercely loyal to her cause. They would fall on their knees to her cousin along with her. She would beg only once and if rejected would go for her throat, no matter if it costs the lives of five thousand men.

She felt her lips and the last kiss of Bothwell that still lingered there. How she ever broke away from his embrace was unfathomable. Now she must be brave and follow her own lead without him to guide her. How had their plan failed so miserably? It had been falling apart in front of her eyes for months.   She realized her only hope was held in the hand of her southern cousin who she did not trust and truly wished to remove from her throne. Life was becoming more complicated and dangerous and not even the sound of the gentle current could lull her to sleep.

Instead she thought of how she will inform the English that Darnley was attempting to kill her. That is why he was found in the garden trying to escape. Cecil had the drawing, this was evident. He or one of his henchmen had lit the gunpowder. She doubted if he had ever lit a candle. She must convince Elizabeth she would never risk losing her son or hurt his natural royal father. While her cousin sheltered the exiled lords that murdered Darnley, she learned of their hatred for her husband. Elizabeth will take to her bed, as she is famous for when she is in a quandary. The outcome will be a wise decision, helping an anointed queen can be the only outcome. It will benefit her reign. There is no room for treachery in Elizabeth's court. Always she will blame the lords. She hated Darnley and his Lennox parents. They had a legitimate claim to the throne and it scared her. Lady Lennox was in the tower more than home. Darnley's father was a hated relative exiled to Scotland. Elizabeth would realize that Mary brought balance to Scotland. The kind only a true successor can bring. The only way Elizabeth would kill Mary is if her own head be threatened. Mary was confident that no one would dare touch a queen with their naked hand yet alone with a sword. Suddenly she felt her second wind and retrieved her rosary beads from her cape and started to pray in earnest.

Chapter 23

Bothwell could not understand how he could be in prison when he must be free. He is shackled like his lover. He was caught escaping from his castle room and now is relegated to a dungeon in Dragonholm Castle. Crouching and cold chained to a fat stone pillar he walks and thinks while the chain links cut his skin like a rusty saw.

Never did he think that Danish women who had followed him around Europe, begging him to marry her, forcing love down his throat, would go to these ends for revenge. I remember no dowry, nor did I abscond with it, as the king of Denmark is accusing. Luckily, he had faithful friends back home who were negotiating his release, but he had no news in months. Others wanted him extradited so he could be tried for Darnley's murder once again. Even this sounded like a good option at this juncture.

How had it come to this? It boggles the mind. He pounded his head with his fist and kicked at a rat scurrying across his feet hungry for supper. Word will soon come. "Each day I shall dig a hole in the wall to make the hour come quicker and document my plight." A grating noise from above spooked the man below and he looked up to greet a ray of light that brought little comfort. The boy was mocking him again pretending to send down a drink. Once again he told the fool of his riches and earldom. Why does he not believe me? "I will make you a rich man if you release me or get word to my men. Free me and my kingdom awaits you. I am the Duke of Orkney, a very powerful and wealthy man." The boy laughed heartily and stuck out his tongue. He spit down into the hole finally slamming the flap into place, forever. Soon he feared he would be feral and insane unable to help even himself. He was haunted by the vision of Mary day and night. His mind played tricks on him and he imagined her in the worst of circumstance. He tore out his hair and howled like a werewolf at the moon, but nothing could settle his mind that was slowly slipping away. He looked up and was so happy to see Mary. She reached out to him with loving arms and a smile that could light up the world. With the last of his vigor he tried to get up and take her in his arms. Thankfully, he fell on his face and mercifully drifted into oblivion.

Chapter 24

The Earl of Shrewsbury's castle was hers now, more or less. Elizabeth had exacted her punishment. Cecil and all of his spies were rejoicing. They wanted her executed for certain, but realized they would be pushing her kinswomen too far to ask just yet. It was a cold and ugly place as were her keepers the Talbots. It is her duty to plot an escape and claim her rightful throne. Bothwell will soon sweep down from the north, as he is its master. A manly husband this time, with a body like armor, she finds herself aroused and laughs for the first time in months. The mirror that decorates her tasteless room still reflects back a face as lovely as a crimson coated sunset. Her face was glowing with the bloom of youth that no one could take away. Her majesty was evident in the aura that surrounded her. She needed no crown to assert her authority and regal bearing that only befitted a true queen. You could sense it when she walked into any room. Her iron will brought subjects to their knees. These plebeians dare not touch or judge her. She was untouchable royalty, still above all others on earth. Unhappily, the spider now had her fly. Elizabeth's web was laden with spies, traitors, pretenders to the throne and fools. Never had she caught an ordained queen, a tasty morsel, usurped by the lords who were glad to stock England's royal kitchen.

Where was the arachnid now? Would her cousin keep her like a jewel hidden away so no other nation would steal her away or worse help her remove Elizabeth, rendering her the only queen on this island. Then she would perform her duty as her ancestors deemed and had for a millennium.

She could bear it no more and lay quietly in her foreign bed, as if in surrender. The last light hurried away leaving long shadows on the wall like a specter. They reminded her of the lords in their dreary black capes and matching tight caps that seemed to squeeze their brains too hard. They wished to say adieu to their true and rightful Scottish queen and be released from her grasp. Never could this be, for kings and queens would have their way with a sweep of the scepter. The night came and blotted out all reason. Mary dreamed again of the Rough Wooing. Henry the VIII had never stopped pursuing her. If he could dig Edward and himself up from the grave he would murder Elizabeth with his bare hands. The king would put Edward and Mary on the throne in a joining of the crowns. How he would enjoy rewriting history in his favor and to his liking, continuing his obsession with the Tudor succession. She awoke in a sweat and cried for the first time since she last held her son at Sterling and that seemed like centuries ago. She was twenty six years old and desired her husband beside her. They could make love and provide more heirs, for this was her duty and rightful role. Luckily, Elizabeth was providing her a semblance of royal luxury and a small court. Yet, she was a virtual prisoner. There was scant allowance for exercise and fresh air.

Luckily, some of the servants seemed to genuinely enjoy that they were serving her. She was especially fond of the eight year old page Anthony Babington, who had pledged his life to her. He had already become a reliable little spy and courier. She would persist and continue her fight no matter what far off castle she was spirited off to against her will. There were powerful allies waiting for her correspondence and from the outside they would devise a plan to join forces and invade England to free the rightful queen. Catholicism would be reinstated and the Pope realizing his folly and her true value would welcome her back into the fold. She would become a saint.

She closed her eyes and thought of Bothwell, facing the truth that she may never see him again. They had loved and lost, for now. She must put thoughts of him on a back shelf and concentrate on escaping or accepting the offer of marriage offered by the Duke of Norfolk. There were rumors that Bothwell was dead, cruelly executed by King Frederick. She placed her hands lovingly upon her breasts and fantasized that they were her true loves. The fact that she continued to have carnal desires was welcome. Outside it was very still. These Midlands were a stale place. They were flat and resembled Scotland not at all. When she looked out of her balcony her view was a disappointment, unless the sun was in exceptional splendor. She never had to work at beauty like this desolate land. It was as natural as a spring shower.

She had noticed how Lord Talbot had held his breath a bit when they met. His wife was a stone cold fish and stood there shooting invisible arrows at the royal guest, that Elizabeth had pawned off on the couple. Soon she would find her way out of this maze and history would be glad.

Chapter 25

Rarely did Elizabeth gaze upon her naked self. Always in attendance the highest bred ladies of the court perpetually fussed over her. Often annoyed at their petty manners she displayed little patience.

She would wallop those little missies if their comb was not gentle or they brought her the wrong necklace. She was a natural loner needing no friends. The only human element she could not rub out was her love for Robert Dudley. She had made him an Earl, bequeathed much land upon him, gave him armies to lead, but she could not marry so loath was she to share her crown. She was glad to listen to his good sense. However, it was William Cecil's word she took to heart. All of her life he had been wise and his advice had lead her to the top of the kingdom, where she planned to stay, alone.

She had taken to her bed, as was her custom when she felt tired and frustrated. She had torn off layer after layer of her ornate gown and thrown it on the floor like it was a rag. Earlier today even her undergarments had given her pain as she made urgent decisions and signed important documents. This nakedness was a feeling of freedom and release from her grueling duties. If only Robert could join her here, the love of her life, it was tempting. She knew that he would never control her with sex as was his heart's desire.

At the moment there were other pressing matters that all of the men in her life were focused on. They all wanted Mary queen of Scots to remain their prisoner or worse. They wished to try her for the murder of that awful Darnley cousin of hers. Without a care they would swat her like a fly and go on with their eternal spying.

Methinks they better provide a better bait. I continue to believe the lords have set my pretty little cousin up. Moray told me repeatedly of his hatred for his brother in law while here in exile. I welcomed him to my court and was entertained with tirades regarding the behavior of that man and how he was harming Scotland. He would love to throw him off his throne. That it seems is exactly what he did when he lit the fuse, the leader of the gunpowder plot. This was her opinion. For this she would not hold or execute her cousin, but if she discovered she was involved in a plot to harm herself Mary would woo the day.

How fortunate The Rough Wooing had failed. Elizabeth may have never reached the throne had Mary born her brother a child. Perhaps they would have become good friends and cousins instead of reciprocal traitors. Yet, they sent each other miniatures of themselves and pretty little letters, but the subterfuge was as thick as bread pudding. Nay, Mary had not the balls to kill Lord Darnley. Nor would she endanger her child by him. Thankfully she had dropped that jewel, James VI, into the lap of the kingdom that may be placed in the crown of England someday. The Rough Wooing had gone round about. It lost momentum, but her father has somehow pulled an heir out of his hat from the grave. If he be raised a Protestant by John Knox and guided by the Earl of Moray he will be in a perfect position to rule. She was well aware that if she did not soon marry he would be the most logical heir. If Dudley did not have hand by now and the crown matrimonial, no man would. But this Catholic queen must be kept down. Those popish ways are not for these times. The monasteries will remain closed. The Mass will be kept in its place. She will be damned she believes a wafer can be turned into God, pure nonsense. Take the middle road Bess. Each man may worship without fear of death, but those who do not abide by the faith of England tread lightly.

Aye, this Mary Queen of Scots was a thorn in her side. She was certain her cousin would use every resource to push Elizabeth to her limit. Cecil is right. She is a threat to the Crown and always shall be.

Elizabeth had not eaten all day and could not imagine taking a bite. Why did not Mary sail off into the sunset with that worthless Bothwell, Duke of Orkney, "Bah!" That outlaw had never been a friend, fighting for Scotland's independence tooth and nail. Often he has displayed loyalty to the French. "Treason I say!" Those two are a deadly combination of beauty and gunpowder that even I might not be able to quell.

Her right side was all pins and needles for lying there so long. Taking a sip of hot milk she realized it had gone quite cold. She tried to bite into her crumpet but the effort was far too great. On top of all this she hated to admit the worst fact to contend with was Mary's daunting beauty. Flawless and natural she needed no wigs and white paste to camouflage pockmarks and weak features. She was said to be most radiant coming home from the hunt, her auburn hair flying and cheeks rosy as a crimson sunrise. Elizabeth's pampering and beauty aids could not raise her to the league of Mary. This was a mighty blow to the vainest women of her day. I wish men would fall at my feet for my beauty instead of my crown. It is bitter in my mouth this serpent of jealousy. It wriggles around and may come out of my royal arse.

Still, if she betrays me as she must, my grasp will take her breath away. If, as Cecil claims, she is conspiring with foreign powers to overthrow and assassinate me I will be forced to sign her death warrant. Should I see her signature proven upon any parchment of treachery her destiny will be out of my hands and into the executioner's.

Tossing and turning she spent the night counting sheep and all of the ways she could send her blasted cousin home where she belonged.

Nineteen years later.

An old woman was how she looked just twenty six when imprisoned for life. Now nineteen more years have passed and all would soon be over. Mary could hear them building the platform for the block that would soon sweep off her regal head. In her final hours she could still hold it high for upon it she wore three crowns of Scotland, France and England. A true anointed queen shall never falter. Her heritage rose out of the ashes of the War of Roses. Her great grandmother was Elizabeth York wife of Henry VII. She sat quietly by his side as he put England back together again. From her she had inherited the great beauty now lost in captivity. Mary was the perfect blend of Tudor and York. Her rose would be a soft pink rendered so by the blending of the red Tudor and the white York rose. She was the sought after prize that Henry failed to seize in his lifetime. It amazed her how the succession had taken a surprising turn, and at the end Henry had cultivated an heir that would be to his liking. His favorite sister's great grandson would spread their monarchial seed across England.

Through her son James VI the true blood of her ancestors would bring Henry's chosen heir to the throne.

Mary was working her long slender fingers like wings as she strove to complete her last tapestry. Upon her death it would be sent to her son King James VI, whom she had not seen in nineteen years. She could visualize his wrinkly baby face like it was yesterday. His warm little body loved to wriggle around in an attempt to get his mother's attention. This was long before he knew himself a prince or king of the realm. He was just a child that needed his mother's love, be she a washerwomen or a queen. At least they shared those precious moments creating a bond that would somehow transcend time.

Laying the work on her lap she took a wig her faithful servant Mary Beaton had obtained. She was the only one of the four Mary's to travel through her twisted life with her. Almost bald one whisk of grey hair remained on a head where the crowns should be. Her legs, older than her years, were blown out of proportion from arthritis. Her castle prisons were not the most comfortable. Always damp and cold one could find mold growing on the Talbot's furniture. Elizabeth allowed her little exercise; fearful conspirators would emerge from behind an evergreen and carry her off to the insurrection against the Crown. At one time she had a full court that mimicked her life at Holyrood. At least there was a time she has been beautiful and sought after. How good it had been to be a lusty woman that relished life. Men had fallen at her feet, not for her lineage, because they desired her as a woman of flesh. She smiled and for a moment an onlooker could catch a glimpse of what had once been the glory of Europe. Removing two letters from her handbag she looked lovingly upon Bothwell's. She would not read it again; instead she gingerly placed them in her terrier's collar. The devoted lass would follow her to the end of her days hiding beneath her dress until her head released its final sigh. One was a final farewell to the cousin she never met. The other, the last correspondence she received from Bothwell eighteen years ago. Most importantly, unlike the forged 'Casket Letters' that implicated them in Darnley's murder, it was authentic. Those damnable lords had gone too far practicing her handwriting and placing felonious love letters in a silver casket box. They made certain it was delivered to William Cecil and Walsingham's men to use against the queen.

Poor Bothwell, he was long ago dead. For ten years he was tortured in Dragenholm dungeon, chained to a stone pillar. In his determination to devise an escape plot he dug a circle into the ground as he walked hunched and miserable in his continual circle of frustration. Feral and insane, he mercifully was released into the light, escaping to the kingdom of our Lord Jesus Christ. The King of Denmark refused to release him, convinced he had an unresolved dowry debt with that whorish woman. Nothing had been proven, yet he remained crouching and howling at the moon like a wild beast. How they had loved one another, but not enough to free themselves from the bondage of their destiny. Perhaps she was errant in her pursuit of the English throne. A quiet and uncomplicated life may have been the sensible choice. Laughing out loud, she realized never could she abide by this. She shunned sensibility. Her future was set into motion when Marie Guise gave birth to a female successor who would be a Catholic queen. Carrying the cross on her back her suffering was meant to return Scotland to the true faith of our Lord Jesus. The only Lord she would have to deal with again and this was a comforting reality.

The room was drafty; she clutched her shawl tightly around her now stooped shoulders. She felt a bit warmer and found the courage to think of David Rizzo. She remembered the night she dreamt of him. His ghost begged her to return to France and the safety of her Guise uncles. Why had she been so rash? Alas! Her youth had been wasted like a newborn fawn devoured by the wolf. Imprisonment had sucked her earthly desires out of her like a bat extracts blood from his victim, yet, she had provided the successor for the throne of both England and Scotland. Her son would reunite

Britannia completing the work she had crafted, even as she languished in Elizabeth's fish bowl.

How many men had died to set her free? The Duke of Norfolk, Elizabeth's cousin immediately pursued her hand upon confinement. He had not obtained permission, believing his royal blood provided special privileges. Elizabeth was furious. Eventually he rebelled, attempting to join forces with Spain, hoping their combined power would place the newlyweds on the throne. But Philip II never arrived. He watched the fog roll over an empty harbor that was the port to his execution. The duke was beheaded, another souvenir for Cecil and his spies to gloat over. Other heads fell and rolled while the next brave man stepped up to take his place.

Poor Anthony Babington, the adorable page boy who greeted her when she was forcefully brought to Shrewsbury's Castle. He grew up to be her greatest, handsome champion. Now he lies drawn and quartered in a traitor's grave. This final conspiracy had been conceived and weaved by Walsingham, her majesty's spy master. He set up a scam to convey Mary's letters, setting up a trap that led to the block she would lay her head on today. Ultimately, she had signed a letter instructing her fellow conspirators to murder Elizabeth before they freed her, to ensure her cousin could never ensnare her again. It also laid out details of the number of forces needed for an invasion and what ports would be of best use.

Sadly, she had failed in her efforts to destroy the rebel lords at Carberry Hill. Mary knew then she was doomed. Never would they relent in their pursuit to punish her for marrying Bothwell. Running to Elizabeth had been like jumping from the fire into the cauldrons of hell. Now she was knocking at death's door.

Fotheringhay Castle was the palace Elizabeth had chosen for Mary's trial and execution. It was another remote destination lacking glamour and appeal. Surrounded by a double moat and river it was like a natural clamp. To the very end Elizabeth was determined to keep a tight leash on her captive. Mary thought of how the last three years became insufferable. Every day she felt as confined as a canary whose owner continually provides a smaller and smaller cage. Since the assassination of William of Orange three years earlier by a zealous Catholic, her life style declined rapidly. The last vestiges of court life were ceased. A few loyal servants remained, skeletons to tend to her ill health and base needs. Her laundress and coachman were forbidden to speak; for Walsingham was certain these were the avenues of her treasonous ciphered letters. The smallest pleasure she received giving alms to the poor was cut off and it was this seemingly insignificant punishment that hurt her the most. She now realized there would be no leaks unless Walsingham designed them. A horrible man, Paullette, was assigned to make her life miserable and her isolation complete. The bars to society were closed as fast as the impenetrable gates of hell.

After the William of Orange incident thousands signed a radical oath to harshly punish regicide. The fear wrapped around and around Walsingham and Elizabeth like a snake strangling its victim. Mr. Secretary of State was always against her easy keeping. Paulette, was the perfect solution. He was an extreme Puritan and had no sympathy in his cold and cruel bones. He followed his orders with complete precision not deviating a royal inch.

Mary laughed to herself when she remembered the bonds that men had signed to depose Elizabeth and set up a Scottish queen. How Walsingham and she had fenced for years. Finally he plunged his sword into her heart. He had devised a system that outmaneuvered her every move. Touché! Even the poor local brewer was unaware that the letters in the bunghole of the barrels he thought he was sharing with Mary's loyal men were actually agents of Walsingham's. Letters traveling to and fro were being read and Walsingham was privy to all. The letters to the French Embassy, with skillful ciphers may as well have been posted on the streets of London. Mary shook her head like an old elephant when she thought of her foolishness in believing that her beer barrel scheme was foolproof. She had been overjoyed to find a clever venue for her favorite pastime - spying. Luckily, she had not endorsed treason when years earlier Throckmorton communicated with her in a plot to kill Elizabeth and invade England. Regardless, his execution tolled the beginning of her end. Luxury and freedom were bygone and her suffering began in earnest.

The trial commenced in September as she watched the landscape change like the seasons of her life. The green leaves, full and vibrant, slowly gave way to the colorful death of autumn. The executioner, snow, now has effectively lopped off all of their heads, soon to be caught by a chilly wind; they are carried off to judgment day. How ironic she is meeting her death in February, the same month of Darnley's murder. A sad hour is approaching and she will yield to the cold winter of her misfortune. The solstice has passed as have her hopes.

Mary's faraway eyes looked back over the years Elizabeth had allowed her to conspire and plot. The Virgin Queen was fearful of the repercussions inherent in authorizing the death of a truly anointed queen like herself. Self-serving decisions were made by her with only her welfare in mind. But her minions had gathered around and rooted out every stick of evidence striking Elizabeth again and again. For three days she laid awake refusing to take her pen to the death warrant. At last she was weakened by the pecking of her council. Mary knew Walsingham had a pet name for her, The Bosom of the Serpent. Her spies continually reported the minutia of court gossip and the slanders against her.

Mary could not deny her life had been focused on regaining her rightful throne. Day and night the plots continued against Elizabeth's reign. It was her life's work and for that she would gladly die. Mary closed her eyes for a moment and let the sun gently stroke her face. It was warm and comforting transporting her back into Bothwell's arms. His manhood pulsed against her warm body and she rejoiced in the forbidden pleasure they shared for such a short sweet time. "Nay!" She would not trade a moment, all were her choices.

No one ruled her. Elizabeth tried, but by killing her she was raising Mary to the level of martyr and she knew it. Soon she will kneel bravely, placing her head just so on the block that the ax must fall but once. When she tumbles her scarlet undergarment will be revealed for the entire world to witness. Her message would be clear. Though she be a martyr her beginning would be revived when James VI of Scotland is crowned James I of England, avenging her life and death.

Epilogue 16 years later

The Year of Our Lord 1603

The elderly queen stood in front of her favorite window for days aware that she was dying. Elizabeth thought back on her life in which she was a princess then no longer a princess, thrown into the tower by her sister, Mary I. She believed Elizabeth had conspired in a plot to usurp the throne. Finally she was found innocent and released. Otherwise, her sister would have had her beheaded. Death was a fearful thing at such a young age. Soon William Cecil came to her as she sat under the hearty oak tree to announce she was now Queen of England. After being rightfully brought to the throne she would love Robert Dudley above all other men, but not her Crown. Now her heart sank when she remembered caressing his face lying fully dressed in her great canopy bed. All of the curtains were shut and for a while duty was forgotten.

No one need remind her of her greatness. She left a mark on England and her rule was long and glorious. She had sacrificed Robert Dudley for her country and she must not regret this now. For a moment her eyes became wide as she thought she saw Robert coming towards her from the knot garden. Although she knew him long dead he was moving quickly as if in his youth. Looking closer she shuddered and wailed, for instead it was the Grim Reaper and soon he would be upon her.

She still clutched the letters in her hands, signed Mary Queen of Scots and true successor to the English throne. What a stubborn brat she was to the end. Well, two could play that game as Elizabeth refused to break their seal until her dying day. When the executioner passed them on to Cecil and him to her, they were buried in the bottom drawer. Now their contents had spilled out like her guts. The first letter her cousin left her was a personal farewell; expressing sorrow they had never met. Yet, it was the second missive that had given her more pain than seeing the approach of the Grim Reaper. It was an authentic love letter from Bothwell that had not been among the casket letters so crucial in acquiring a conviction and execution. She had never believed a fig in those forgeries. Only Mary's signature on the plot to dethrone and murder her had been the deciding factor bringing her plume to the death warrant. Never had she believed Mary had a hand in Darnley's murder. The lords were obviously guilty in her mind, using her cousin as a pawn. But, as she read the short and precise words it was as if one-hundred tiny arrows pierced her heart. It read:

Dear Heart, My Mary,

I bow to you and would have killed a million men just to touch your face of Venus once more. God help me if I do not find you in this world. God will reunite us in heaven for he knows you are the rightful queen who will rule eternally.

Our love and your beauty have no boundaries. Together they will break our early shackles and free us to embrace immortal. I love you and beg forgiveness. Never harbor regrets for our earthly actions against the abomination Darnley. Think only of our love and ponder upon no sorrows for ours is a higher place and I long for us to be there.

Forever I shall be your devoted subject and husband.

Farewell, Bothwell.

The letter dropped in slow motion to the floor like a whisper: followed by Elizabeth and James VI of Scotland now James I of England ruler of the greatest kingdom on earth, son of Mary Queen of Scots.

THE CELTIC TREASURE

Chapter 1

Londinium, present day London, 60 AD, burned to the ground the day Boudicca, Queen of the Celts continued her revolt against the Roman invaders. You could see the fire for miles and for days black soot fell back to the earth. Clouds above were grey and hanging very low. Angry and heavy, the sky had to blindfold itself against the carnage that was raging across the countryside below, as a rabid bear looking for lost cubs. Here and there you would see a singed Roman sword or shield, the eagle half burned off of its once majestic perch.

Boudicca stood at the lookout her troops had erected. Satisfied the battle was won she stepped back into her chariot. Although not tall her might was found in the hardness of her cat-like, marble eyes and lips iron clad from years of determination. The Romans had turned her into this hard, unreasonable woman who ruled with a whip of triad knots and an iron fist.

How foolish her husband King Prasutagus had been to trust these egocentric animals that had assured the Celts that they could keep half of their land. How dare they double cross her! She raised her voice, yelling to her top general, "Panzer, let us now hunt them down like the dogs they are. They dared rape me and flog my daughters. I shall impale them and tear them limb from limb with my bare hands. Rome shall fall and the Celtic nations will rise from the ashes of Londinium. We will come back here and make this the center of our government. It is a good place. I like it here and I am a queen who chooses where my castle will be built." She urged her magnificent horses with beautiful braided manes forward, followed by two hundred thousand troops consisting of men, women and children. Her third victory was a sign the gods were on her side. The number three was a very significant digit representing much to the Iceni people. Victory was assured. Her commanders formed a wing protecting their queen and headed in the direction of the final battle.

Thirty miles away where the fleeing Roman army was taking refuge, General Antonius Marcus Tactirius knew he had barely escaped the wrath of Boudicca. Had he not been informed by his scouts in such a timely manner his legions would be dead or at best scattered over the countryside. He had miraculously saved a semblance of the army. His military skills were superior and he had stood out at the academy in Rome.

How had it come to this? He thought about her lovely curves and raven black hair. Instead of a crown she wore a decorative helmet. He remembered when they made love she insisted on keeping it on her head. How she glowed in the candlelight, keeping the tent so warm with her hot blood and fiery eyes. But it was her lithe muscular body that supported her youthful breasts that kept his manhood at attention.

He thought of his Roman wife Julia, so reserved,

even in the bedroom. It was not that she was not tender. Her shyness somehow worked its way to arouse him. She would gently spread her wings and quietly place his sword of flesh within her. But never did she look at him. Instead she would whisper his name until the matter was closed.

Boudicca, however, rode him like a mighty horse. "Behold, upon me she rides and the pleasure is unimaginable." With wide eyes open and cunning she dares him to orgasm before her time has come. He capitulates to her every desire. They perform acts that Julia would not dare entertain.

Antonius had come to her camp after her husband's, the king of the Celts, death in order to negotiate a peace treaty. He was hoping that the emperor of Rome would see reason and spare the Iceni for much good would evolve out an amicable relationship. Unfortunately, the emperor did not care for their destinies to be intertwined. Instead they were to be eradicated and cut down like a human harvest for Rome to feast upon. The Iceni would be conquered like all other nations that Rome set its far reaching eyes upon. Boudicca's twenty tribes would surely be conquered. Each and every one would fall like Jerusalem, Gaul and Egypt. The world was theirs for the taking. Emperor Claudius had actually rejuvenated interest in Britannia. After the death of Julius Caesar there had been a decline in the occupation. But Claudius was determined to ensconce Roman troops there when he thought of the riches and military benefit of that island country. General Antonius was supportive, but he felt they had gone too far when they attacked the Druids at Anglesey. Boudicca was now meting out her revenge on Claudius. She had by now sacked Camulodunum, Colonia and Londinium and was blazing a path with 200,000 hornets towards Verulamium. Close to eighty thousand Roman soldiers were dead. Tonight Antonius would sleep and in the morning search for her. That would be easy considering the size of the army she had amassed.

Chapter 2

Boudicca was satiated. She felt as if she had eaten the hearts of a legion. Her scouts had spied Antonius riding hard toward their camp. Obediently, they informed her of every move a Roman made. They reported him riding north carrying a white flag. Boudicca said, "Leave him to me, and do not interfere. He is coming to try and reason with me. I shall torture him for information and then slit his throat. I will let him know that heaven is on the side of a religious vengeance. I would die myself rather than be his slave." As she spoke these words they resonated around the council like a druid priest performing a ceremony on the equinox. But inside she could not deny that she was deeply in love with a Roman, the greatest sin she could ever imagine. She longed for his life not death.

A few hours later she was resting on her lush pile of furs in private quarters. She had to touch herself only once for a moment when she thought of him and her organ quivered bringing her the full impact of his sexual powers over her. She could climax just thinking of his rippling physique like the rough mountains of her homeland. His handsome face rose like a deity over the expanse of his god-like being. He must be the incarnation of Adonis as I am of Morrigan. Suddenly she started beating her fists against the bear rug and pulled at her scalp wailing. She knew it was to no avail. He was the enemy and she was Queen of the Celts. Her husband had been a weak man giving into the foreign pigs' demands. However, she would eat them for dinner. She must suppress her wild, outlandish lusting for a man she can never have, but would always love.

The cold air was creeping into the tent under every crack it could find. Winter was coming as fast as the battle ahead. Soon they would find the remaining demons somewhere in the forest and destroy everything in their path. The sacrifices they had made will bring famine. This year's crops had been neglected. The Romans had burned the fields that remained. Yet, they would survive. Her leadership would give them resolve. Every muscle ached. She could tell where each one was. It was like she was more than one woman cut up into quadrants and small pieces of pain and weariness. She had let herself fall into the abyss of deep rest where the blackness brought relief from the task ahead. She would let herself slip into the void, surrender only to nothingness. Then she would descend into Hades bargaining her soul with the dark creatures who ruled the underworld, all for the heads of the Roman Empire on a clay platter.

They threw Antonius at Boudicca's feet and kicked him heartily. They ordered him to kiss the feet of their reigning leader. They were filthy and smelled like moss. None-the-less Antonius got a twisted pleasure out of the perverted act. He dared not look upon her until she commanded him with her voice of pumice and honey. She sounded like a plebian washer woman, but once he laid his eyes upon her, the power of her physical beauty and natural leadership brought him to his knees. He would make love to her on a bed of nails, if that was her desire.

Boudicca's simple tent had been hastily erected as a temporary headquarters for her top ranking soldiers, if you could call them that. The majority looked like scarecrows stolen from the fields they labored in. Weapons, mostly homemade, were the butt of jokes around Roman campfires. They were no match for the Roman machine that ate greater numbers than this for breakfast, in Carthage. How easily the enemy capitulated to the superiority that was inherent in Roman citizenship. It was more precious than gold and was dispensed to a privileged population who took full advantage of its pleasures. Rome was at its pinnacle. Antonius believed that Caesar, Pompeii, Gaius Marius and Sulla, all dead, had taken the empire to its height. They looked down from their own Olympus, now smiling, and sanctifying the acts of an army led to a future of aggression. To possess was to be Roman, but to be possessed was slavery. The only image above Rome was Boudicca's, for romantic love was paramount in its pursuit to replenish the earth.

She kept him on his knees for over three hours without uttering a word. She ate a great dinner of venison and roots, chewing like a piglet, burping and throwing pieces of fat at him. After combing her long mane, with not a care in the world she relieved herself in the corner. Little did she know how the training of this soldier was no less rigorous than that of a Spartan. He could stay there for hours while his mind wandered to Sicily or Tuscany. His mind had always been his greatest weapon. His heart, now that was his Achilles heel.

Chapter 3

The night arrived with starry eyes and harvest moon. Boudicca looked at Antonius and could stand it no more. "Rise Roman and let me look upon my enemy so I can further enjoy victory." Antonius got to his feet and before another aggressive syllable was emitted he grabbed her in his arms and pulled her hair as hard as possible, with no mercy. Before she could object they were rolling on the dirt floor.

He kissed her, sending his tongue down her throat like a Roman sword. Boudicca went wild and bit his lip until it bled onto her own. She clawed at his face and tried to kick him between his thighs of steel.

Although her guards were just outside she did not utter a sound. He ripped off her loose garment and took her breasts into his hands like he owned them. They never failed to fascinate him. For the next four hours they could not stop. All of the battles and horrors had turned them into sexual beasts. They were afraid to stop for death was everywhere and this was the best place to hide.

Chapter 4

Once they were calm Boudicca told him of her love for him. She wanted Antonius to help her lead against the Romans the next day. The Celtic people had every right to throw out the foreigners. This was their land since time out of mind. She would not think of conquering Rome. With this, Antonius threw back his head and laughed so loud the guards came tearing in. She quickly commanded them to return to their posts

Chapter 5

Gauis Suetonius Paulinus, the commander in chief for all Roman legions, threw the plans for battle to the ground. The day had been a grueling march, covering fifty miles of rugged Celtic terrain. Give me the Apian Way, the Forum, the altar of Mars, civilization at its best, he thought. His eyes, black as coal, were mined by a long line of imperial generals. His grandfather had been second in command to Gaius Marius and his mother was related to the Caesars. Patrician blood flowed through him like the Tiber through Rome. He towered over most men. Although not classically handsome, women swooned when his powerful charisma overtook their sensibility. However, he had little time for romance and was satisfied with an arranged marriage that left his coffers overflowing. He rarely thought of Claudia and relieved himself with lusty women whenever he chose.

He forced his mind back to the arduous task of defeating two hundred thousand rabid, infested, rock throwing, and hatchet wielding Celts who recently devastated more than half of the occupying army. Hours no longer mattered. He could remain awake for days when he was hungry for barbarian blood. Camp was falling into its own rhythm and familiar sounds. There was precise order in a Roman war camp and twice so in a desolate outpost such as Britannia. He must cease being so prolific in battle so he can get demoted and sent home! Unfortunately, to disembark from this savage place he had to crush the savages. Now! Today! He pounded his fist so hard against the map he broke his favorite ring. Luckily, it was not the one that housed the imperial seal. It exacted the ultimate authority in this far away realm. He was Commander in Chief and no one would defy him. He was growing wealthier each year. Soon he would retire to Capri. He could see the two famous rocks jutting out of the sea like beautiful breasts. They rose out of the water and the splendor of the moonlit night illuminated the scene he imagined before him.

All of his plans had to be delayed because of that she-devil, Boudicca. He would kill her himself. She must be captured and made an example of. This was his preference. He would have every man in the legion rape her after he had exhausted himself, of course. He had been told of her legendary and fiery beauty. He would bring her so low her bones would crush beneath his boots until they were dust. The plan was simple. The Celts, so certain of victory, would find them. But he would choose the place and time. Preparation was everything when losing and the tide must turn. He knew her scouts had done an excellent job locating his camp. He had all the horses and equipment lined up facing south toward a thick forest and tight gorge that would serve as a natural shield. There was no doubt his plan would eliminate the enemy once and for all.

For hours, they had practiced the maneuvers that would overcome the unbalanced numbers of seventy thousand Romans against two hundred thousand, give or take a few useless Iceni. Tactics and superior weapons would win and destroy the motley creatures. They would dig their own graves and jump in if they knew what was in store for them. Those savages were bringing down modern civilization. They would like to move us back to the dark days before the Empire ruled, he thought. Eradicate the lot and the world's intelligence would increase dramatically. He picked up his red cloak swinging it about like a hatchet. Placing it on his back he went outside to sound the trumpet of terror that would lead them against the angriest mob that had ever threatened the ancient world.

Chapter 6

Boudicca's hoard would terrorize the bravest army. The men were stocky and had wild, unruly hair. Some wore helmets with huge horns sticking out. With faces painted to imitate the dark creatures of the underworld or forest you could smell them five miles away. Many of her followers by now had no shoes, and their clothing was in disarray and beyond repair. But tonight they seemed as if in a trance. A hoard of Celts lay under the stars that would bring them luck and fortune. They knew all things were written above. It was the gods' ways of communicating. They were all created out of darkness and fire. The gods must be appeased and the Roman pagans expelled so they could return to their fields, and this they would do at all costs. So both sides prepared for the largest insurrection against the mighty Roman Empire in any of its provinces, ever.

Chapter 7

Spent and sweaty Boudicca stretched like a sleek cat that appreciates her own luster. Nuzzling against a very manly arm she felt if it was to be her last day on earth it will have been worth it. Suddenly she screamed for the guards and had them tie poor, naked Antonius to the center wooden pole. "Leave us now less I bid you to enter."

Once they were alone she plopped down beside him like a common farmer's wife. "Listen to me, you must. Number one, I love you. Number two, you love me more. Number three, you must understand the moral implications. Would I sack Rome? Why did you come here if your country is so bloody special? I would not leave my forest domain, which is surrounded by the pearly sea. What a jewel she is and the treasure is mine not Rome's. You can keep your decrepit Coliseum and filthy markets. Try hunting for food lest you become weak. That is why we are defeating you. This is our land of Druid worship and ancestral rites that will protect us against any storm that rages against these shores. I beg you accept this armor of conquest I offer. Besides, if you do not do as I say I will have you drawn and quartered. A little trick I learned from my Roman enemy. Then I will cut off your head and place it on a stick for all to see." Inside she knew she would never do such a thing. She would prefer to take her own life for her feelings were genuine and ran as deep as her royal ancestral blood. Suddenly she shivered and remembered the soothsayer's saying of how you shiver when a hawk flies over your grave. Now she knew exactly what that meant.

Chapter 8

She left him there for a few hours to think and make his decision. She catnapped and dreamt of the triple dyad. It was the symbol of her tribe who was far superior to the Iceni. She and her daughters represented the new and living Celtic Triple Goddess. The legend that was so basic to her religion. The three goddesses linked with the other crucial dyad land, sea and sky. Together they ruled the world in harmony with natural forces. But now their entire civilization was being insulted by forces that were uprooting their very existence. Boudicca would have been surprised to know that the number three had religious, mythological and magical associations worldwide. The Three Furies, the Trinity, the Three Headed Hounds of Hades and the Three Wise Men were just a few. These entities are usually related to life, death, rebirth and back again.

What she did know is that her people believed that she was the resurrection of Morrigan, the Goddess of Battle. She wore her trinity belt locked with an interlaced double triguetra. This was her ultimate symbol of sovereignty. The Cross of Triguetras never left her neck. Antonius loved how it laid between her breasts and swung like a pendulum when they made love.

As a child she had been taught to form the eight-knots essential to Celtic culture and religion. Her bowls, cups and torches she made herself using intricate knot patterns. The knots with magical powers she engraved on a special vase over which she performed her incantations. Inside the depth of the clay pot the gods of the forest listened and decided the fate of her requests. The Druid priests had passed down these chants and other stories of the gods and goddesses. Boudicca knew from their prophecies that she could turn herself into a raven and hover over the battlefield. For now, however, she would pray to Alator, the god that nourished her people. This she understood to be the cause for which she was fighting.

When she awoke she felt rejuvenated. She took a moment to examine the series of triple spirals that decorated the inside of her war tent. She said a few incantations and felt the gods were with her. Now she was ready to face Antonius. She would bend him to her will.

By now Antonius was tested to his limit. During his ordeal he could not help being worn down by the truth in her words and his desire to live and die by her side. This combined with her overpowering sexuality and beauty was making him weak. She must be an incubus, but his common sense did not seem to care. Let Boudicca fling me to the underworld with her. There, I will taste her lustful lips that look so hard but are surprisingly tender. The dimple on her chin marks her a she-demon. Yet, it makes her face so much more interesting to look upon. Combined with all of the sharp angles, chiseled cheekbones and perfect nose, any man would fall under her spell. Some things she said made sense. They would rule together if they won the impending battle. If Paulinius is crushed the Emperor will not return to this faraway place. It was forgotten before. History does repeat itself. Just ask the Greeks.

Suddenly he saw her rise from her furs and it was like a siren calling him to the rocks. He looked into her wicked emerald eyes that at that moment were the same color as the mystical forest of Ur. There was no need to speak. Boudicca threw on her garment and helmet calling for the guards. "Bring this man something to protect his body and feet in battle." Before they returned they made love hastily, for they needed their strength for the most important battle of their lives. Antonius knew the might of the Roman army on the worst of days and he felt an eagle circle over his grave.

Chapter 9

Paulinius had his army ready every pila, arrow and sword. They drilled over and over. Step, lunge, pull back, and discharge. Those in the rear line change to forward. Step, lunge, pull back, and discharge. The archers flexed their bows until their arm muscles enlarged before their eyes. Paulinius was never satisfied. Soon they would give the rag tag Celts the frontal attack they longed for. Let Boudicca believe that his troops are trapped. Soon they will all be under his boots and Rome will rule here for a millennium. The mighty pila, which resembled a javelin, will force the Celts to abandon shields from the sheer weight of the weapon. They would be exposed and easy prey, with nowhere to go, but Hades. His sagittarii were a special regiment that had come from the cream of the ranks, sent by Rome to halt the insurrection. They would shower the onslaught until the pila would give them a blow they could not anticipate. Two thirds of all the archers marched while the remainder rode on horseback. These equestrians were a new development in warfare and were powerful against an impoverished army driven by patriotic ideals. The Roman Republic would come at them with the speed of an untamed beast.

Chapter 10

The West Midlands had a thick forest where a narrow gorge led into an open flatland that went on as far as the eye could see. The Iceni scouts had reported watching the Romans disassemble their camp and head towards Cutter Mill. While the Romans were busy oiling their war machine Antonius knew what he was up against. He used all of his military knowledge to help organize the massive, pathetic regiment that was relying heavily on his skills.

As Boudicca was finishing her last chalice of wine she thought of her weak husband King Prasutagus. He had won his independence by leaving his lands jointly to their daughters and the empire, but when he died there was only betrayal. Boudicca hated all the emperors, especially Claudius. When she learned they had erected a temple to him at Colonia she had it burned to the ground, starting a rebellion that came at the Romans like a blizzard. Today it would finally end. She longed for peace in her heart and a home for her people, where they could enjoy the rest of their lives in comfort and happiness.

When the queen set foot outside her tent, the warriors saw she had painted her face blood red and black, in the style of the triple spirals. She sent for Antonius and commanded her advisors to march toward the West Midlands. Upon their arrival they would place the wagons and other carts in a semicircle in order to trap the Romans. The old people and children could watch the slaughter and pass the story down for generations. There was no doubt their gods would provide the just revenge that was their inherent destiny.

Boudicca called for a group of musicians to play a warrior ballad with their flutes, drums and feadon whistles. She asked them to continue playing until they were victorious. Antonius had passed out all of the Celtic long swords to only the most skilled and experienced warriors, for there were limited weapons. Most soldiers in the ranks came from their farms with sickles, pitchforks, hatchets, rock slings and other rudimentary weapons. It was through sheer numbers that they would win this day even against Rome's unparalleled arsenal.

Boudicca had her chariot fetched and she rode to the head of an untamed sea that looked ferocious and mighty, able to devour everything in its path. She raised her whip of knots that were detailed in the triad spirals. Antonius was beside her on his white mare. His face was also painted and he looked as if he were Iceni. Only his family signet ring would provide a clue to his identity, for he would never abandon his father's gift. Her resolve was now his. He rode toward his destiny like a ship running with the wind. It was blowing with a vengeance tipping the craft like the scales of justice in their favor.

The frontal attack was now in full force. Behind them the wagons were secured in a tight circle.

They could smell the Romans beyond the gorge that was now in their sight.

The forest was their intimate friend and they hated the vermin that was invading and polluting its majesty and wonder. Boudicca thought of all of the innocent creatures that must be scurrying from the impending violence. They were certainly scattering, running for their lives like they do when they see the smoke of a forest fire.

It was past midday and the sun seemed liked a friendly deity. Boudicca released a rabbit from the fold of her war dress and watched as it ran toward the gorge. This was a traditional divine act and signified a good omen for it sanctified the direction of the battle. After this divination Boudicca and Antonius prayed together and waited for the enemy to show himself. In a cold and bitter war cry Boudicca, Queen of the Celts and legend of ancient folklore raised her whip. She commanded the demonic mass to march forward and bring this rebellion to fruition, so she and Antonius could return to Londinium and build the mightiest kingdom in Britannia.

Chapter 11

Paulinius had his legions ready as never before. Every man had been well fed, rested and drilled within an inch of his Roman life. It was a sunny day, which was a rarity in this dismal land of incessant rain and depressing clouds. They seemed like funeral veils. He was glad for a good slaughter. It would be like a Greek play. Tragedy was always awaiting a soldier in some form. It was tragic this episode had not ended sooner.

The Prefect at Legio would be sorry he had not sent reinforcements. He had better fall on his own sword before Paulinius laid eyes on him again. It could have been such a simple slaughter. Now they were forced to do double duty. No matter, they would be victorious. Mars shined in the sky last night winking at him. He passed on the mirth of a warrior god who would always reign supreme over barbarians who worshipped false spirits and goblins.

Paulinius waited until the sun was behind him. It was one of the basic precepts taught to him at the military academy. He strategically placed each man three feet apart. Each rank was separated by six feet. This tricked the enemy into counting greater numbers. The infantry was kept in the front lines. The cavalry was kept in the rear to prevent anyone from escaping into the dense forest. Horsemen were always secondary in battle. As commander he tried to place himself in the right wing and today he would do so.

He had gone over all possible tactics in his tent deciding on the wedge. It was a commonly used tactic used by attacking legionnaires. A triangle was formed. The front tip went to one soldier who held a sword toward the attackers. Small groups were now able to thrust well into the enemy. Hand to hand combat would be difficult for the putrid Iceni. This is when they would brandish the short gladius, a small thick sword. It was very useful for low thrusts that could devastate a man below the belt. It ripped out his intestines with an agile cut and pull. They had lured the foxy queen into the tightest trap of her life. There would not even be time for her to chew off her own limbs to escape. He would break the enemy line. There would be no opportunity to change tactics. With unmatched discipline the Roman fighting machine waited for Paulinius to sound the trumpet. Not until then would they charge, unleashing the fury of the greatest military force on earth. An eternity later the sound rallied the men to move quickly as the standard bearer lead them forward. The standard bearer carried their emblem high above the red wave of Roman tide that was about to make landfall on a beach that would soon be soaked with blood. When the men saw the symbol of the eagle spreading his wings in glory they understood the majesty of Rome and their mission. Rome would rule the world for it was written in the stars.

The two armies knew another prayer would not

save them. They could stall the force of time no longer. The greatest insurrection against the might of the Republic had begun. The screams, grunts and crushing of bones could be heard for miles. The ground shook like an earthquake. It could split wide open and eat up both forces. Roman archers spewed their arrows before the barbarians had a chance to kill one soul. They fell from their wounds like a herd of deer hunted by starving men. Next, the deadly pila was deployed. The javelin crippled men when they were forced to abandon their shields from its sheer weight. Naked and vulnerable they were now easy prey for all combat weapons that were flying in their direction.

Boudicca could not believe how effectively her army was being decimated before the battle even began in earnest. Unbelievably, not one Roman had sustained a mortal wound while her troops were falling like flies. Paulinius was a patient man and waited for the opportune instant to send out the wedge formation that would soon crush the entire flood. The sounds could now make a man deaf. Decibels broke all records and the noise level rose to inhuman proportions, like something you would hear in hell. Some men defecated on the spot out of mortal fear. Holy terror surrounded the battlefield like a formation no general could mimic. The first soldier's gladius now plunged into a boy of sixteen who had dropped his weapon. He fell to his knees like a rag doll as they lopped off his freckled head. Doomsday was upon them as the wedge opened up. Hand to hand combat would be the deciding factor of whose gods would be appeased. Blood spewed out over the monstrous mayhem inciting more violence. Arms were scattered here and there and severed hands insisted on clutching their useless weapons. The Roman wedge performed its duty by the book and effectively cut down the enemy. The harder the Celts fought the more the Romans cut them to pieces. Strength and power grew with every drop of blood and ounce of pain they inflicted, sucking life out of everything that crossed their path. A million Druid incantations could not reverse the spell in the Celts favor.

Boudicca and Antonius were starting to comprehend the enormity of their predicament. Fighting against his conviction, reason coaxed Antonius to advise his lover to retreat. If they saved a semblance of their army they could return and fight another day. They would go into hiding and rise again when the gods would renew their strength and resolve. But it was too late. The oppressors were moving forward like an avalanche. The wagons they had lined up around the site were impeding escape. The slaughter had now started in earnest. Bodies were piled on top of each other. Cries were cut off in an instant as heads toppled onto the blood soaked field. Intestines were being rubbed into the ground that felt like quicksand thick with human innards. Women dragged their children by their hair in a feeble attempt to continue living. Old men fell to their knees hoping for mercy but were met with the end of a sword that knocked them out forever. The Romans were the sickle and it was the Icenis' last wheat harvest that was trampled and wasted. It was no longer needed to feed the population that Paulinius had snuffed off the face of the earth.

In the confusion Boudicca could not locate her daughters. She had to support their desire to fight in order to set an example for all the other families. Several of her high priests and generals spirited the exhausted leader and her renegade towards a designated location. They had selected this spot with great consideration in advance. Although she did not believe it was necessary, she was not opposed to a sensible back up plan. This is where they had also hidden the Celtic treasure that had been amassed over many centuries and passed down from dynasty to dynasty. They were determined the Romans would never take possession of it even if they destroyed Boudicca.

Epilogue -- Year 2064

A hiker seeking shelter from a violent English thunderstorm stumbled upon the Celtic treasure and remains. He noticed a large boulder disturbed by several earthquakes over a thousand years. He used his thick walking stick as a fulcrum and found a cave filled with stalactites and stalagmites that looked like witch's teeth.

Using his laser flashtube that lit the room like a noon sun he found a few large, jagged rocks that had fallen out of the wall. There in the quiet soothing darkness he saw what looked like a hinge and part of a chest. It seemed very old and he would stun the world with its dating and authenticity.

Archeologists called this the greatest find of the twenty first century. A previous discovery of similar magnitude was discovered in the nineteenth century by Heinrich Schliemann, a wealthy German interested in archaeology. He discovered the Trojan treasure, in Turkey, after working for decades, bogged down by a Turkish government that thwarted his efforts at every turn. It had been a grueling job. They had no patience for his expedition and he had to apply a Herculean effort to fulfill his vision.

But this newest discovery just fell into the archeologists' lap. They had carbon dated artifacts and applied the latest methods of dating, recently invented by a rising star in the field. They knew within months when some artifacts had been crafted. Also, the bones that had been interred were easiest to identify. From matter extracted from the orbs of the male skull they had determined he was of Mediterranean origin, most likely a Roman. The female was a Celt of middle age adorned in jewels and wearing a bronze helmet. It was decorated with the triad symbol of the Celtic goddess. They were convinced it was Boudicca and the buried Celtic treasure. It was no longer a legend.

The male was heavy-boned and displayed injuries sustained by soldiers in battle. His skeleton had chipped bones and a healed tibia. A broken collarbone was probably sustained from the last blow he received in battle.

The cave was not far from a famous battle that took place in 60 AD. Twenty years before, archaeologists had unearthed the site, bringing back to life the genocide that brought the Iceni to their end. It was the ethnic cleansing of its day, willfully wiping out a people with no regard for their religion, culture, age or gender.

History repeats itself, in order to tests its students' understanding of the lessons. Unfortunately, humans are errant and the schoolmaster must get out the hickory stick and strike the same wound over and over again. Compliance is something they fight against and certainly do not relish. Humans must be beaten down for centuries into obedience until eventually they rise like walking dead and repeat the mistakes of their ancestors.

Curiously, to reinforce the scientific data, a simple signet ring sanctioned the outcome of the tests. For upon the Roman male's left hand, it still circled his boney finger. It bore a symbol that was surely his family crest. An eagle soaring in the air followed by a raven bathed in the powerful Roman sun.